The **What**'s **Drama,** *Malibu?* **Bennet**.

MICHELLE GAYLE'S career has spanned TV, theatre, film and music. She was first known for her TV appearances, which began in the 1980s with children's drama *Grange Hill*, followed by *EastEnders*, before she moved over to a glittering pop career that saw her achieve six top twenty hits and sell a million records, most successfully her 1994 single "Sweetness". Michelle has since appeared on TV shows such as *Doctors*, *Holby City* and *Family Affairs*, and she starred opposite Ed Stoppard in the 2006 film *Joy Division*. In recent years Michelle has presented on *Loose Women* and also taken part in reality TV shows *Come Dine with Me* and *Dancing on Wheels*. Michelle lives with her husband and two sons in west London.

oh. My. Days.

breathe

My life is non-stop drama.
Looking back, I guess it all started with
THAT paparazzi shot.
But that wouldn't have happened had
STEPHEN not thrown that punch.

You could say he wouldn't have done that had
I not met ROBBIE twot-face WILKINS.
And the reason I met Twot-face was
because of... Hmm, MALIBU.

Uh-oh, methinks there might be
something going on here.
Why does trouble literally begin and end
with my sister, Malibu Bennet?

Love
REMY x x ☺

The What's Drama, Malibu Bennet?

MICHELLE GAYLE

WALKER BOOKS

First published 2014 by Walker Books Ltd
87 Vauxhall Walk, London SE11 5HJ

2 4 6 8 10 9 7 5 3 1

Text © 2014 Michelle Gayle
Cover photographs © 2014 PLAINVIEW / Getty Images, Lise Gagne /
Getty Images, Anthony Lee / Getty Images, Antonios Mitsopoulos /
Getty Images and Brian Hagiwara / Getty Images
Cover and inside illustrations © 2014 Paula Castro
Cover design by Walker Books Ltd

This book has been typeset in Fairfield

Printed and bound in Great Britain by Clays Ltd, St Ives plc

British Library Cataloguing in Publication Data:
a catalogue record for this book is available from the British Library

ISBN 978-1-4063-3935-2

www.walker.co.uk

For Tony, Isaiah and Luke

This is the diary of
Remy Louise Bennet,
the one dependable
thing in my life!

P.S. Malibu, being my
sister DOES NOT give
you licence to read this!

Remy + Leonardo DiCaprio,
always & 4ever! 😊

Remy ♡ McFitty

Channing Tatum
– Phwoar!!

<u>Monday 29 July – 3 p.m.</u>

Hi guys... I'm back! Did you miss me?

Mum's just been up to see me.

"How are you, sweetheart?" she said, tilting her head sympathetically.

I. HATE. PITY.

But since my meltdown last week – on only the biggest TV breakfast show in Britain! – I don't want Mum worrying that I'm a headcase so I said, "Fine. Just need to get some sleep."

Usually she'd screech something like, "*Sleep? At this time?*"

But instead she just stroked my head and said, "Yes, I'm sure you do, honey." (Clearly, does think I'm a headcase.)

Oh well, could be worse. I could have spent the whole day in bed sobbing or cringing – or my new one, crinsobbing (a combination of the two). But no, I'm v. proud to say that for the first time in a week, I, Remy Louise Bennet, have been out. Yay!

Went to see a psychiatrist: boo–oooo!

Yep, I finally caved in to the powers that be: namely my agent, Harry Burton. I did it so that the bigger and, more importantly, RICHER powers that be (those that provide serious wedge for my Terri Catalogue clothing range) will not drop me. All I need to do is show them that I'm "fixing" myself; that their celeb "fashion designer" is not meltdowning EVER AGAIN. But believe me, I'm so embarrassed about said meltdown that a part of me would rather be dropped. Actually, I'd rather not show my face in public for the rest of my life and just stay in bed crinsobbing! But when I called Dad he said earning this kind of money at my age is a godsend. Especially when there are people with top-notch degrees that can't even get a job in Mickey D's.

"Just give it a try," he said.

"Why – do you think I need fixing, Dad?"

"Erm... I suppose everyone does, in a way."

Obviously, he also thinks I'm a headace. ☹

My psych is called Dr Stephen Clein. He assesses all the contestants before they go into the *Big Brother* house. Spent half my session trying to get some info out of him – like "Did Jasmine really like Lee or was she playing a game?" – but his lips were properly sealed. Told me nada.

Said he'd protect me in the same way too.

"What's to protect? I've already shown myself up on national TV."

"And now seems the perfect time to talk about it," he replied.

That's the kind of link presenters make on *The One Show*: "*Aha! And speaking of embarrassing moments…*" But it's not a poxy TV programme, is it? This is my life!

"I'd rather not, thanks."

He tried to coax it out of me. "I've heard all about the incident. I believe you've been referred to me because your reaction was out of character?"

"*Very,*" I replied. "I mean the only person who might've seen me flip like that is Mum, when I'm premenstrual and she has done my head in."

"Hmm. Embarrassment is understandable but can you explain what made you so angry?"

Told him I didn't want to talk about it. But the answer was no. And the worst part was that I could feel the anger building up again. It scared me. The whole thing scares me… If I'm honest, that's the real reason I decided to see Dr Clein. Just being in his office, talking to an actual shrink, was majorly scary. Luckily, he realized that and stopped pushing me. He's asked me to write down what happened instead – blow for blow. He wants me to add how I felt at the time, and how I feel about it now. Then I have to take my account to my next session.

So, here goes…

THE 100% TRUTH

I'd felt nervous as soon as I'd opened my eyes that morning – first appearance on live TV and all that. Those nerves doubled when I got to the studio, and went into the stratosphere when I was waiting off set (just out of view) and I heard the voice of Mum's favourite TV presenter: Lorraine Macintosh. I swear Mum was more excited about me meeting Lovely Lorraine (as she calls her) than she was about me being on TV.

"Now, my next guest was thrown into the public eye when her boyfriend, footballer Stephen Campbell, fought her *ex*-boyfriend, teammate Robbie Wilkins, during a televised match..."

WTF?! I was so annoyed.

Every interview I do brings up the Robbie business and it winds me up, big time. Come on, guys, it was a whole year ago! Why couldn't "Lovely Lorraine" have mentioned how well my salon, Tah-dah!, was doing? Or have focused on the launch of my autumn clothing range, which was what I was there to promote? I'd even kitted myself out in a "Remy L.B. by Terri Catalogue" dress: green velvet, fitted to the waist, then flared out into a tutu. (Very fashion!)

"... so, please welcome to *Good Morning A.M.* ... Remy Bennet."

I began the strut I'd practised with Malibu the night before. (She'd lifted it from Naomi Campbell on *The Face*.) I executed it perfectly; was genuinely thinking my big sis would be proper proud, right before I tripped over a camera cable, went flying and landed on the floor – green dress over my head, matching green thong exposing my bare bum cheeks to the nation. Aa–aaaaaaaaah! ☺

Wanted to die of embarrassment. Almost did, but something – maybe the cameraman's grin, the fact that I was STARVING from the crash diet I'd been on (had to look good for my first live TV appearance), or the discovery that Lovely Lorraine was just as bad as everyone else who had interviewed me this year (oh, and way smaller than she looks on TV, by the way) – SOMETHING made me lose it.

"What you grinning at, you *cringe* *sob* *cringe*? And as for you, Lorraine *mothersobbing* Macintosh, you can just *sob* off. (Decided to keep this clean for you, Dr Clein.)

Anyway, that's basically why I need to address my "anger issues", as my official statement (that I didn't actually write) said. And I might have sounded a bit attitudey in your office today, but I do know there's no excuse for shooting my mouth off like I did, and I'm almost as ashamed about it as I am of my exposing my backside to the world; and the fact that it's had five hundred thousand views on YouTube only adds to my shame. But why, why, why did the *Sun* have to go overboard with its "Bumgate!" headline?! Did I twerk with Santa? NO. And I don't care who their source was – I did NOT do it for publicity.

As for that so-called comedian (refuse to mention his

name) who said the force from my bum's wobbling could have caused an earthquake ("Can you imagine – death by bumquake!" he joked), there is a special place for you in hell, my friend.

The End.

<u>3.20 P.M.</u>

PS Forgot to say that Dr Clein isn't as bad as I thought he'd be. He says he just wants to improve my self-esteem, and then the "managing anger" bit should take care of itself. To help, he wants me to start each day by telling myself: "I am Remy Louise Bennet. I am not perfect. But I still love being me."

When I asked whether I could add, "With a tiny bit of lipo, I will love myself so–o much more," he sighed and said, "No, Remy." *boo*

Oh yeah, he also thinks I shouldn't have stopped writing in my diary. It's been a whole year, I can't believe it; but things went cra–azy when I appeared on the front page of the *Sun*, and after that I didn't have the time. Well, I'll have to make some because Dr Clein says it's a good way to get things off my chest. He reckons I'd been bottling everything up and then released it all on the *Good Morning A.M.* cameraman and "Not-so-lovely" Lorraine. Methinks he might have a point, so here is said diary... Tah-dah! ◄ (See what I did there?) ☺

Gr–rreat. Just checked Twitter. Have tons of replies to my "I'm back! Did you miss me?" tweet. Loads of "Welcome back" etc. But just as many "Who cares?!" and "No, we didn't!" Also found a couple of joke accounts: *@Bumquake-Remy* and *@Remysbuttcheeks*. Twitter = #selfesteemfail

Tuesday 30 July – 7.05 a.m.

I am Remy Louise Bennet. I am not perfect. But I still love being me.

Hmm… Personally, Dr Clein, I could think of much better ways to start the day, all of which involve STEPHEN. And I'm up at early o'clock to look as good as I can for my Skype date with Mr McFitness himself. ☺

Blow-dried hair: ✓
Applied bronzer: ✓
Added copious amounts of mascara: ✓
Twenty-five minutes to go. Woo-hoo!

8 a.m.

Was lovely to talk to Stephen all the way over in Tokyo city. He's in Japan for a pre-season tour and it must have been doing him good because he looked proper hot. Everything was one notch better: his hair, his body, THOSE lips.

"How have yer been, gorgeous?"

"Not too bad, considering Harry made me see that psychiatrist," I grumbled.

"It's just fer show though, right?"

"*Yeah*, of course."

"I mean, what yer gave that cameraman and Lorraine MacShort-ass was an average bit of hairdryer treatment."

("Hairdryer treatment" is what footballers call it when their manager starts screaming in their face when they've not played well. Which happens a lot. Fact learned from Google five days ago when Stephen first mentioned it.)

"Oh yeah. It was totally average," I agreed.

Luckily, Stephen left for Japan the day before *Good Morning A.M.* He only saw what happened on YouTube and so far he's always tried to be really positive about it.

"OK, I understand it's embarrassing but just think how yer'd feel if yer didn't happen to have the best bum ever seen on TV," he said after he first saw it. Followed by: "To be fair, that Lorraine 'Edinbugger' Macintosh probably deserved it." (Edinburgh isn't popular with Glaswegians.)

With Japan being eight hours ahead and him busy travelling, training and playing, I'm not sure how many "Bumquake" jokes he's heard either. I was just wondering whether I should get the worst ones out of the way, to prepare him, when I spotted his roomie Oscar Raymond in the background.

Oscar's American and he's become Stephen's closest teammate. He's super-square and slightly gullible, and we love winding him up.

"Do you love me, baby?" I said, suddenly putting on a cute voice.

Stephen made a sideways glance at Oscar, and twigged. "Aw yeah, I love yer loads."

"How much though?"

"Aw, up to the moon and back – easily."

"Ahh." I started making loud kissing noises. *mwah, mwah, mwah*

Stephen put his face close up to his computer screen until he was practically snogging it: *MWAH, MWAH, MWAHHHH*

"Hey buddy," said a majorly blushing Oscar, "do ya need me to leave the room?"

"Naw… I think you'll be all right." Stephen's big cheesy grin gave it away (it's taken a while for Oscar to adjust to our sense of humour).

"Oh right. You're just throwing the piss, huh?"

"I think yer might mean *taking* the piss there, dude. Now behave yourself," Stephen said to me as I cracked up laughing.

"Sorry, Oscar – just playing," I called out.

"No problem," Oscar breezed back. "And make sure you call Suzy."

"I will."

His wife Suzy completes the squareness of Oscar's world. I knew she must have been well shocked by my foul-mouthed rant, so I've been avoiding her, even though she sent an uplifting text: *You can get through this – you just*

17

gotta believe in yourself. Ish happens. (She doesn't swear.)

"What time's your match?" I asked Stephen.

"Five-thirty. We've got to leave in a minute."

"OK. Well make sure you bloody score, then."

He smiled. He's had a brilliant pre-season so far. "Yer have such a way with words."

I smiled back. "Can't wait to see you tomorrow, baby."

"Aye, me too."

6.45 p.m.

Well, my second day out of the wilderness was full-on. Harry called at 8.30 a.m. and I swear he didn't take a breath for a whole hour. Said he'd found the perfect person to rebuild my image: a PR woman called Camilla Douglas-Smith.

"What's wrong with Mandy?" I asked. I like the PR woman we've been using so far.

"She ain't right for this. Camilla's in another league. I've arranged for us to take 'er to lunch."

"When?"

"Today?"

"But I wanted to spend the day in the salon! I owe my beauticians that after staying away for a week."

"The salon?" Harry repeated as if he'd never heard of it.

"Yes, Harry – *the salon*. The salon that I own."

"But you've got a four o'clock meeting with Terri Catalogue."

"Yeah, I know. I plan to be at the salon until then."

He gave a theatrical sigh. "I can't begin to tell you how important it is for you to meet Camilla. It's the only slot she's got. And if anyone can get rid of your 'Bumquake' label, it's her. She could convince people the sky's green."

I was sold. "What time?" (Getting rid of the "Bumquake" label is a major priority.)

"One o'clock at Scott's in Mayfair."

"See you there."

Got to the salon at 10.15 a.m. and Lara was running the place like clockwork. Felt like they hadn't missed me at all. (Slightly annoying.) Lara and Charlie didn't mention *Good Morning A.M.* but neither of them made eye contact when I spoke to them. I suppose they're embarrassed for me. (Even more annoying.) Not like my very-to-the-point "Catalan *not* Spanish" beautician Isabel, who said, "Wow, I saw de YouTube. I don't think your bum was all dat wobbly. In fact in Catalonia we would say deese eese—"

"Isabel!" Lara interrupted hurriedly. "Your client has arrived."

The good news was that every beautician was fully booked. *Kerching!*

Got a taxi to Scott's in Mayfair and arrived bang on time for my meeting with Harry and Camilla Douglas-Smith. Never been to Scott's before. It's proper plush, full of suits, and when I saw Camilla I decided that she must have chosen it. She's way more posh than Mandy, the "lives in Windsor Castle" kind of posh that I've only seen on TV.

Camilla doesn't say "of course", she says "of caws", and "yah" instead of "yeah". She's a middle-aged blonde with a pinched nose and three children: Octavia, Sebastian and Tristan, who all ride a "haws". She says that she's going to kick "some proverbial ahse" for me.

"And will you stop the press calling me Bumquake?" I checked.

"Of caws. I intend to rebrand you. By the time I've finished, your name will be synonymous with clahss."

This all sounded great to me. Then when we left, Harry told me her fee.

"Five hundred pounds a week?!" I gasped.

"She's worth every penny. 'Ow many people do you think would 'av already sorted a top interview for you before you'd even signed a contract with 'em?"

He had a point, but I only agreed to a month or two, as I'm not made of cash. Going to do the "top interview" and photo shoot with *Here* magazine tomorrow.

Had some time to spare before my meeting at Terri Catalogue's Essex headquarters so browsed the shops for a bit. Bought my little nephew a cute T-shirt that says **My Mum Rocks!** and myself some control pants (seeing as Dr Clein says liposuction is a no-no). Also tried on a few dresses and decided that, from now on, black is the best colour for me – the black ones all made me look slimmer. The others – ugh!

As I left the last shop, two men in football shirts passed me in the street and then turned back to point.

"Is it a bird? Is it a plane? No, it's the Bumquake!" one of them shouted.

Ha. Frickin'. Ha. Thought about swearing at them, but as I'm rebuilding my image and all that, I told myself, "I am Remy Louise Bennet. I am not perfect. But I still love being me." Then I dug my teeth firmly into my tongue and showed them a middle finger instead.

Need to put this Bumquake crap to bed. As soon as. Hope this Camilla's as good as she says she is.

My Terri Catalogue meeting was with Annouska Hemmings – the *real* designer of the Remy L.B. clothing range. As soon as I arrived, Annouska hit me with a bombshell opening statement: "This season, red will be the new black."

"No. I can't wear red. I'll look like a bus."

I don't know why, out of lack of self-esteem maybe, but I was fishing for a compliment. Something along the lines of: "A bus? You? NEVER."

Annouska said, "Not a chance… The photographer will stretch the picture to make you look slim."

8.30 P.M.

Hey Twitter folk, some breaking news: red is the new black! #RemyLB #TerriCatalogue

Just took Mum and Mal to see some flats I like. First thing

Mal said was "You'll make it easier for Stephen to not commit if you buy a flat."

"*You're* the one who said it would make him pull his finger out if I told him I was buying one!" I replied.

"Yeah, but I didn't tell you to *actually* buy one."

Aa–aaargh!

Good thing I worked out a while ago that it's best not to take advice from Mal – a little something to do with her "Who's the daddy?" drama.

She must have been reading my mind. "Anyway, it probably isn't worth listening to me any more."

No shit.

Mal thought the first flat was the best. It's a swanky one-bedroom place on the top floor of an eight-storey building that's literally five minutes away from Mum's. (V. handy if I want her to keep doing my washing and ironing.) ☺

Mum preferred the second, which is more like twenty-five minutes from hers. "It may be smaller but it's in a better area," she said. (Methinks she wants to avoid doing my washing and ironing.) But she probably does know what she's talking about, seeing as she's watched every episode of every property programme at least twice. "They don't call it *Location, Location, Location* for nothing, you know."

Will wait and see what Stephen thinks. Made an appointment to take him to see them tomorrow night.

Was trawling through YouTube comments about my "bum flash" under my fake name, Romano Di Caprio, when Malibu came in, just as I was typing *You don't even frickin' know Remy!*

"I don't know why you do it to yourself," she said. "They're all losers. Now come and say goodnight to Junior."

"Junior" aka my baby nephew, Gary Johnson Junior, is small but surprisingly strong. I went to Mal's room and bent down to say, "Goodnight, chunky monkey," but he replied with a head-butt to my right eye. Ow!

Apparently it's Alan's fault. Whenever Gary Junior has a bad night, a knackered Malibu hands him over to a knackered Mum, who then hands him over to Alan. Alan must still be on Australian time because he doesn't moan about it. Instead, he says, "I'll take him to the front room and find something to watch."

I used to think *Ah—hhh, how sweet* – imagining Junior's surrogate grandad enduring *Bob the Builder, Peppa Pig* and *Tweenies* – but stopped wasting my breath when I found out that he then sits down with him and watches three of the most violent sports on the planet: ice hockey, rugby, and Aussie Rules Football. Now, Gary Junior tackles, bites or head-butts people at will. And his dad, Gary Senior (used to be known as Goldenballs but they're more like lead now), is proper pissed off about it. SO AM I.

Right, that's it. The pain's too much. Going to have to ice my eye. ☹

Eye is still throbbing. BAD.

One more sleep till I see Stephen. YIPPEE!

Wednesday 31 July – 8 a.m.

I am Remy Louise Bennet. I am not perfect. But I still love being me.

Woke up thinking today's going to be a good one: my McFit comes home from Japan! Then went to the bathroom and looked in the mirror – my eye looks like I've been sparring with Mike Tyson! WTF?!

8.30 a.m.

Had a few strong words with Malibu. "I've got a photo shoot today and your son's blooming given me a black eye!"

"He was just playing."

"That's not the way normal kids play."

"*Normal* kids?! What're you trying to say?"

"I'm not *trying*, I'm saying it: one-year-olds do not go around head-butting people. *Fact.* At this rate, he'll be expelled from nursery the first day he walks in."

"He'll probably stop doing it by then."

"He'll *never* stop if you keep letting him get away with it!"

Then she started to cry and Mum, who'd just come out of the bathroom next door, rushed into her room asking what the commotion was. Malibu said I made out that she's a crap mother.

"What? Check the T-shirt I bought him – My Mum Rocks!"

"And what do you want – *an award*?"

"I can't win," I huffed as I walked out.

Mum followed me to give me another talk.

"New parents are very sensitive," she said. "You have to choose your words carefully."

"Fine. But when 'Baby Psycho' hurts someone else, don't say I didn't warn you."

"Shu–uush. She'll hear you," Mum whispered, then added, "I think she's post-natal."

I'm the one who should be depressed, after the week I've had – although, to be fair, even after *Good Morning A.M.*, I wouldn't swap with Mal. She's the one sleeping in a cramped bedroom with her "challenging" baby son while Gary Senior hums and haws about whether he wants her back for good. Apparently he's still finding it hard to get his head round her cheating on him with Lance. Last week I told her that as his mum's a Christian, she should teach him how to forgive.

"But who's going to teach him how to forget?" she replied.

8.45 a.m.

Yippee! Stephen just landed and called me straight away. He wanted to meet up for lunch, but I can't because they've set aside 10 a.m. till 6 p.m. for the *Here* mag photo shoot and interview. Looks like Camilla's really pulled it out of the bag. Apparently it's going to be a double-page spread and, as Ron Burgundy would say, that's "kind of a big deal".

Arranged to meet Stephen tonight so I can show him the flats.

Dear God, please let him see sense and ask me to live with him instead. ☺

7 p.m.

Strange day.

Used to get proper excited about photo shoots – loved getting my hair and make-up done by professionals. But the shine soon wore off. Well, I got butterflies over today's shoot as if it were my first. This was important: the fight back from the brand new, sophisticated me – a chance to bury Bumquake FOR EVER.

The glam squad did their bit – clipped in a few extensions, concealed my black eye, shaded and highlighted my face to make it look like I had amazing cheekbones. It may have taken ninety minutes but I did look ten times better. Then a stylist called Fran turned up with a clothes rail full of dresses, jeans and tops – a mass of blues, pinks and reds.

I used to gasp at the amount of clothes stylists brought along. Today I just said, "Erm... Got anything in black?"

Luckily, she did. My first pick was a black leather dress with white daisies running along the hem. Luke, the photographer, said, "Great dress, Fran," when I came out, as if she were the one wearing it. Then, as an afterthought, added, "You look good, Remy. Right, let's rock and roll." It was time to pose. Eek!

For me, posing always feels awkward. Just can't help it. And if it feels awkward, it looks awkward.

"Imagine you're in a club, yeah, and the lens is... Who d'you like that's famous?"

"Leonardo DiCaprio."

"Yeah. This lens *is* Leonardo DiCaprio."

Awkward.

"Now... Smile... Pout... Make a sexy face, yeah."

AWKWARD.

There was an electronic instrumental tune playing. I'd never heard it before and never want to hear it again.

"Move to the beat, yeah, sway to the... Shall we change the music?"

Poor Luke.

We stopped for lunch. Then Camilla Douglas-Smith called Fran and everything changed. Fran passed her phone over to me.

"Remy, dahling." Camilla sounded even posher over the phone. "I've been sent some of the shots. Now, do you trust me?"

V. strange question coming from a person I barely knew, but she sparked my curiosity so I found myself saying yes.

"Good. Becawse I have an idea that will stop them talking about your ahse, and start them concentrating on your clahss."

"I'm in."

Fran left her half-eaten lunch, took her mobile and walked to another room.

"Yes, can you bike it to me asap?" she said, phone glued to ear, when she came to join us again fifteen minutes later. She ended the call. "New hair," she said to Max, the hair-dresser. "An up-do."

"Sure," he replied.

"And make-up?" checked Bethany, the make-up girl.

"Yes, something a bit softer, please."

She could see me frowning. "Camilla's idea," she explained.

It took an hour to be transformed into a Disney princess. *Is that really me?* I thought when I looked in the mirror – wow! Then the bike arrived and Fran walked in with a WEDDING DRESS. Literally the most beautiful wedding dress I'd ever seen. A mix of cream lace and chiffon – loveliness fit to marry Prince Harry in.

"We're thinking of a fairy-tale bride theme," Fran explained.

Well worth breaking my black-clothes-only rule for. "Bring it on!" I replied.

I reckon Luke still thought my posing looked awkward,

but it felt a lot better for me that time around. At least I managed to smile. It was easy once I pretended it was *my* big day getting hitched to Stephen. #bliss

Then off came the dress, down came the hair, and I was suddenly faced with reality: a five-foot-nothing, leathery skinned journalist named Samantha "call me Sam for short" Turner.

"So, obviously this is your first interview since *you know what*. How are you feeling?"

"Still a bit embarrassed, to tell you the truth – about the fall *and* the ranting afterwards."

"Uh-huh."

She brought up my statement, the one that Harry wrote and released to the press. "You said that you've found it hard to cope with fame and you'll be seeking some professional help. Have you done that?"

I imagined how shocked Grandma Robinson would be to find out that I'm now seeing a psychiatrist. In her day, that probably meant I'd be wearing a straitjacket and locked in a cell with padded walls.

"Um… Well… Sort of. I'm talking to someone. You know, just airing my feelings – I'd been bottling them up."

There. Nothing to worry about, Grandma!

"It must have been hard for you – girl next door one minute, making front-page news the next. *Very hard*."

Tell me about it! Stupid old me thought trying to keep up with the Netherfield Park WAGs was difficult; then I wound up being a celebrity (fully aware that some people would call "celebrity" an overstatement) and realized the real meaning of PRESSURE.

"I never classed myself as a beauty or anything," I explained, "but suddenly people started turning up at the salon expecting me to look like Miss World."

She frowned. "The salon?"

"Yeah. My salon. I own a salon called Tah-dah!"

"Oh yes. Of course."

"If people turned up there and I wasn't looking perfect, they'd actually make comments about it on Facebook or Twitter – sometimes even to my face."

"Any examples?"

"Well, one girl who didn't think I was as pretty as she expected said, 'You're actually quite plain, aren't you?'"

"Hmm." Sam looked sympathetic. "People don't think; and it can't be easy with you dating a footballer."

"Huh?"

"I mean, it's hard enough to keep hold of a rich handsome guy, but a *footballer*…"

Is it me or did Sam for Short ram the pressure up to max right then?

"Yeah… Well…" I stuttered.

"You looked beautiful in that wedding dress today. Any plans you want to tell me about?" she said with a cheeky smile.

"Plans?" I repeated.

"Yes. *Plans*."

I laughed. "Look, we don't even live together, so

one step at a time, as they say."

Sam leaned towards me and lowered her voice. "Listen, as this is your first interview since *Good Morning A.M.*, what Camilla would like me to do is to show that you're moving on with your life. Basically, I'm after a good news story and our audience love weddings and babies."

She sat straight again and raised her voice to normal. "So, do you have any *plans*?" she repeated.

"Er… No… Not really." Sam sighed. I'd clearly let her down, so I quickly added, "But I hope to have some soon."

That made her smile. "And babies?" she pressed.

"What about them?"

"Have they been discussed?"

I shook my head.

She sighed again. "Would you like any?"

"Me? Yeah, I'd like at least two."

Now she was happier. "Good for you. I think you'll make a great mother."

"Thanks. I hope so. I suppose having a little nephew is good training."

"And how old is he?"

"One."

"Ah–hh. Bet that's made you broody."

"Er… Yeah… Sort of."

"When my older sister had a baby, I picked baby names for my own children, even though I didn't have a partner at the time."

We both laughed.

"I've done that too," I admitted. "Maybe it's a girl thing."

"Well… What are they, then? Don't leave me in suspense!"

"Effie for a girl, and Doug for a boy."

"Traditional Scottish names. Oh, they're beautiful, Remy."

I was proper chuffed about this (had put a lot of work into finding those names). Sam for Short was OK really, I decided. If a little nosy.

Got home and when I told Mal I was going to show Stephen the flats she brought up commitment again.

"If he says they're great, you're going to look silly if you don't end up buying one. And you don't *want* to buy one because that leaves him commitment-free."

I thought of the irony of me having photos taken in a wedding dress today.

"What you smiling at?"

"Nothing. Besides, he *has* committed – we're boyfriend and girlfriend, aren't we?"

"I'm talking about taking it to the next level. You know I am."

Anyhoo, I've packed an ickle overnight bag and now I'm off to meet Stephen. Hoping that seeing my potential new flat makes him pull his finger out.

Hi everyone, look out for me in HERE mag – coming to a store near you very soon!

Thursday 1 August – 8.30 a.m.

Had an almost perfect night with Mr McFit. Almost, because the flat hunting didn't get the result I was looking for. He didn't like either of them. *Woo-hoo!* I thought, hoping it was because he had a better idea – like me moving in with him. I said, "Well, what do you think I should do?" with big brown "save me" eyes.

And he replied, "I think yer should hold out for something better, gorgeous."

Grrr.

On the upside, when I took off my make-up to climb into bed, he noticed my black eye, gave it a kiss and then said he quite liked it. "Gives yer a Glaswegian edge."

"Really?"

"Aye. The girls are tough in Glasgow." Then he kissed it again. And again...

1 p.m.

Lunch break. Just waiting for Dad. Think I'm finally ready to meet him, answer questions about *Good Morning A.M.*, and deal with any disappointment he might show in his face. Managed to block twenty-five trolls on Twitter this morning. They took issue with my tweet about *Here* mag. *Would rather set fire to my own eyebrows than read about a Z-lister like you,* said one. So I then tweeted: *Everyone's entitled to an opinion but*

33

not every opinion is entitled to count. This got even more abuse, e.g. *Like yours, you useless b*****, so I had to block another thirty. Deleted the tweet to avoid getting any more. All in between running reception at the salon. Yet again, every beautician is fully booked. Yay! Lara says we could make the Tanarama booth available twenty-four hours a day and still have a queue out of the door.

There's been loads of gossip flying about today because a customer called Debbie Wyatt is on the warpath: her husband has been having an affair with one of our other customers, Natalie Roberts. #scandal

Debbie was in for a mani-pedicure earlier. (Natalie had better be scared because Debbie does kick-boxing.)

"You're well rid of him, Debs," said Charlie.

"Yeah, you're far too good for him," Lara chipped in.

Think that's what I missed most when I stayed away last week: at the salon we're a team; and every woman who steps through the door gets our support. That doesn't seem to exist in the celebrity world.

4 P.M.

Every girl should have a dad like Reg Bennet. The first time he'd seen me since *Good Morning A.M.* and as soon as we sat down to eat he said, "I want you to know that I'm very proud of you. Always have been, and always will be." What a dude. ☺

"But you must feel a little bit embarrassed about what happened," I said.

"You could never embarrass me, Remy."

Dad said I should accept what happened and learn from it. "It'll only make you stronger. And if you gain just one per cent more confidence, that's a result."

"Do you think I lack confidence in myself, then?" I asked him.

"I think, for a long time, you felt you were in Malibu's shadow," he replied, which is so–o true. It's proper hard having a beautiful sister. I then asked how it was going with Elizabeth, and Dad said he's enjoying it but she wants more, now that they've been seeing each other for a year, and he's not sure about making a bigger commitment. Ugh! What is it with men?

Camilla phoned when I was on my way back to the salon.

"I hear the interview and photo shoot went splendidly well, yah?"

"Yeah. Happy days."

"A couple of things, dahling. First, there is a charity ball that you need to be seen at tonight. It would be wonderful if you could get Stephen to tag along. Could you do that?"

"Should be able to."

"Fantastic! And second, the reason I need you to be seen is becawse I'm working on booking a huge TV interview for you."

Eek! TV *again*! It seems so soon!

"A big interview?" I asked cautiously.

"Not big, dahling – *huge*."

"Who with?"

"Aha! That would be telling."

Afterwards, Malibu said Camilla would have to tell her everything, even her sexual history, if she were paying her five hundred pounds a week.

"She works for *you*, remember."

Anyhoo, now wasn't the time to be worrying. Phoned Stephen, who agreed to come with me to the ball. Then ten minutes later, one of Camilla's assistants called to say a top designer was going to bike over some options for me to wear. All I'll have to do is tweet about them.

Now home, waiting for them to arrive. Please let them be VERSACE!

<u>5.20 p.m.</u>

OMG. OK, they're not quite Versace but they've only blooming sent over dresses from Nancy Scott! She's the real deal: Coleen Rooney, Cheryl Cole *and* Victoria Beckham have been pictured in one of her dresses. Woo-hoo! Mal said Camilla must be proper connected to set that up.

I tried on every dress – there were five of them – but that was just for fun because I knew I was going to pick the black one.

"I prefer the pink," Malibu said.

But I'm going to be papped, I thought. *And when my butt appears in some magazine I'm sure the trolls will diss the size of it, anyway, without it being draped in a load of pink sequins. That would only encourage comparisons with Peppa Pig.*

Right, better do my job.

Really looking forward to rocking @NancyScott tonight at the Aid for Children Ball!

5.45 P.M.

DISASTER. Stephen has texted to say he can't come after all. He thinks he's got food poisoning – he's been sat on the toilet for an hour. Poomageddon!

I wrote back: *Wish I could be there to look after you, baby.*

And he replied: *No, you don't. Trust me.*

Hmm. Will have to go to the charity dinner with someone else.

Who though?

6.15 P.M.

Malibu's coming! First, she checked that Mum would be OK to look after my "energetic" nephew. Then she climbed into the Nancy Scott pink sequined dress to see how it would look. Amazing. No one would ever think she had a baby a year ago. (Trust Mal.)

"Don't you just love it when a plan comes together," she

said, striking a pose. It's her first girls' night out since Gary Junior was born, and she's so happy to be coming that I wouldn't be surprised if I looked under her bed and found a voodoo doll wearing a kilt and sitting on a loo.

"Will you still do my hair for me?" I asked.

"Don't think I'll have time now I've got to do my own."

"But you wouldn't be going if it wasn't for me!"

"That's just being selfish!"

Grrr.

Mal's so much better at hair than me. I'll probably look crap now. An ace hairdresser offering mates' rates is what I need. And, of course, I used to have one till we had an epic fall-out. Really need my old BMF James back in my life TONIGHT!

Out tonight with my big sis, all in the name of charidee.
Thanks for the amazing dresses @NancyScott #woohoo

10 P.M.

I'd take Poomageddon over tonight's charity event – every time.

Climbed into my new tummy-control pants then squeezed into the sequined black dress. It fitted like a second skin. *Wow!* I thought when I stood in front of the mirror. For the first time ever, my stomach looked completely flat – no annoying little bulge to hold in when someone was taking a photo. Yes!

We were travelling there in style: Camilla had arranged a chauffeur-driven shiny black Mercedes. Malibu was so chuffed when it arrived. She gave me a high-five.

"Tonight's about letting your hair down," I said to her with a grin, "and you have my permission to get legless. Me and Mum can look after Gary Junior tomorrow, if you have a hangover."

"Thanks, Rem."

When I asked the driver how far away we were and he said we'd be there in eight minutes, I began to get nervous.

"Do I look all right?"

"Of course you do," Mal said.

"What about my dress? Does it *really* suit me?"

"How many times do I have to tell you? Yes—ss."

"You sure?"

"Absolutely positive."

There were a string of black Mercedes clones in front of us, slowly trickling along until they reached a grand hotel with a red carpet out the front. Each would then stop, its well-dressed passenger would step out, and a flash of camera bulbs would go off, courtesy of the photographers lined up on both sides of the red carpet. This was it – the reason Camilla Douglas-Smith wanted me to come; the reason Nancy Scott was so willing to lend me a £2,000 dress. My stomach churned.

We hit the red carpet. Photographers were barking, "Remy, look at me!" *Flash!* *awkward* "Down here!" *Flash!* *awkward* "Up!" *Flash!* *awkward* "Look right!" *Flash!*

v. awkward And so–oo embarrassing!

Malibu loved it though. She posed her socks off until one of the organizers came up to us. "Isn't Stephen Campbell here with you?" she asked me.

"Um… No. He was meant to come but he's sick, so I brought my sister instead."

The organizer looked disappointed. "Right. Well in that case, can we get Remy on her own, please?" Malibu went bright red as she walked to the side and waited for me. I felt bad for her, and it was way more embarrassing posing on my own too. Then finally it was over. Phew! We were escorted through a lobby (where a glass of champagne was practically pushed into our hands) and shown to our table. Four guests were already seated there. I recognized one of them: Dynamic – the magician that looks and dresses like Eminem. He was sitting next to his glamorous girlfriend: huge breasts, tiny waist.

"Hi, I'm Remy," I said.

Dynamic looked down his nose at me. "Yeah, yeah, I know who you are."

"So do we, and we love you," said an immaculately dressed man sitting opposite Dynamic. He looked much happier to be graced by my presence. "I'm Stefan, and this is my hubby, Robert Fitzgerald," he said, indicating an equally immaculate man beside him with silver cropped hair and beard. "I think you're sitting with us."

"Great. This is my sister…" Malibu had been by my side, but had disappeared. Didn't take long to spot her though. She was standing by a waiter holding a tray of champagne and I watched as she took two glasses of bubbly and downed them, one after the other. OK, I said she should get drunk but not in the first five blooming minutes!

"Can you excuse me for a second?" Went over to Mal and grabbed her arm. "Come on, let's sit down." She thought about it, her eyes fixed on the remaining three glasses of champagne on the tray.

"Guess what, we're sitting with Dynamic, *the magician*."

"No way!" That got her moving.

"Sorry about that," I said as we returned to the table, and introduced Malibu to Stefan and Robert.

"Ooh, you're a bit of a silver fox," she said to Robert. "And as for you," she said, waving at Dynamic, "has anyone ever told you that you look like Eminem?"

His slow nod told me he'd heard it a thousand times. Moving on, he politely said, "This is my girlfriend, Lisa."

"Wow, I'd never put you two together in a million years."

I'd forgotten how embarrassing she could be when she'd had a few.

To break the tumbleweed moment, the Silver Fox said, "Love what you're wearing, girls."

"Thanks. They're by Nancy Scott," I told him.

"Only on loan though – we've got to bloody return them tomorrow. Get our pictures taken in them, *promote* her, then she blooming well wants them back!"

Robert saw me cringe. "It's OK, I know how it works. I'm a TV producer." He reached into his jacket pocket and gave me his card. "Who's your agent?"

"Harry Burton."

He nodded. "Yeah, I know Harry. Are you happy with the way he's ... handling things at the moment?"

I blushed. "Yeah. Well ... sort of. Obviously it's a bit tricky with—"

"Look, I've worked with people who have done far worse things than you and bounced back." He mentioned a children's TV presenter who was sacked when he was papped with a dodgy-looking "roll-up" in his mouth. Three weeks later he started presenting an adult show and has never looked back.

"The point I'm making is that you have a window – a very small time frame, but a window nonetheless – where, if you get it right, you'll move onwards and upwards."

Now, if Camilla Douglas-Smith had put it like that, I would have liked her on the spot, I thought, smiling.

That's when Tamsin Spader turned up.

I *love* the way she dresses. She's the latest it-girl model and she's married to the coolest DJ on the planet – Chad Spader. But he wasn't with her tonight. Instead, Tamsin had a tall black woman with huge curly hair by her side.

"That's Tamsin Spader," Stefan whispered. "If I remember correctly, she's sitting next to your sister."

Well, that would have been interesting if Tamsin had actually sat down, but she didn't. She stopped a few metres away from the table, looked horrified, and then walked away.

"Oh my–yyy God. Did you see her face?!" Mal said. "Dynamic, can you pass me that bottle of white, please?"

"Erm… Let's go to the toilets first," I said quickly.

"Ugh! Do we have to?"

"Yes–sss!"

We walked by Tamsin on the way to the loos, and overheard her ripping into the same organizer who had made Mal step aside on the red carpet.

"The magician's cool. But there's no way I'm sitting on the same table as *her*."

"I'm sorry, Mrs Spader, I didn't do the seating plan."

"Well, who did? Because they should know I wouldn't want to sit with a nobody WAG, or whatever the fuck she is."

Stormed into the loos and spent ten minutes in the cubicle, trying to collect myself, with Malibu standing outside it, turning the air blue. She wanted to wade in and give Tamsin what for but I told her not to – I was in enough trouble already. Besides, I'd done my bit and had my photo taken so I decided to make it easy for everyone.

"Let's go home," I said.

Stayed quiet on the drive back and just nodded when Malibu kept going on about what a bitch Tamsin was. "Don't take any notice of her – she's probably jealous."

But jealous of what? She's the cool one; I'm the loser who's now known as the Bumquake. ☹

Friday 2 August – 8.15 a.m.

I am Remy Louise Bennet. I am not perfect. But I still love being me. (Sort of.)

Cried myself to sleep. Why do people like Tamsin Spader enjoy making other people feel like crap? That's what I'll be asking Dr Clein in my next session.

Rang my McFitty just now to see how he's doing. He always makes me feel good. He sounded drained. Said he was up all night but thinks the worst is over. The club have given him a couple of days off training and he's going to stay in bed watching films, in between downing cups of Dioralyte. I told him I'd come over after work. I'm spending the whole day at the salon today.

"How was last night?" he asked.

"Rubbish."

"Bet you looked great though. Even with the black eye."

"It's actually more bluey-green today."

"Aw, even better."

Wish I could take him with me everywhere. ☺

Stick with the people who make you feel good, and ignore the haters! #realtalk

8.45 a.m.

Harry texted to say he's emailed some red-carpet pics of me from last night. He said that they're great and he expects

44

one to appear in today's *Metro*. Felt quite hopeful till I saw it. Papers like the *Metro* don't bother with Photoshop – it's the real you. UNFORTUNATELY. ☹

Now running late. Wonder if Lara will tell me off? Wouldn't put it past her. LOL!

4 P.M.

DRAMA at the salon. There was a fight! Debbie Wyatt (the wife) walloped Natalie Roberts (the mistress) into next week. The police had to be called and everything.

As we were witnesses, all of us were interviewed. Apparently either Debbie had been staking out the salon or she had been tipped off.

"Did you in any way, either accidentally or deliberately, let Mrs Wyatt know that Mizz Roberts would be here today?" PC Adams asked me.

"No, absolutely not," I answered.

The fight's been the big talk in the salon. Every client seems to know about it before they've even arrived, but they still fish for more details: "Where did she hit her? How hard?!"

The general verdict seems to be that Mizz Roberts deserved it. (Clearly, salon community love doesn't extend to mistresses.)

Anyhoo, spent the first half of my lunch break talking to my bestie. Kellie's just got back from what sounds like a full-on holiday with her uni friends.

"Guess who I got off with?"

"Who *now*?"

Can't keep up. Kellie and her new mates get up to all sorts, even when they're supposed to be studying. She's especially close to a girl called Rebecca who – and I never thought this could be possible – makes Kellie look like a nun! I don't like her one little bit but don't feel I can say that to Kel.

"Uni life sounds like one big shagfest slash piss-up," I said. "So make the most of it because real life is hard."

She chuckled. "Yeah, right. You haven't got a *real* life either. You're being paid a fortune for pretending to design a fashion range."

Kellie always makes my situation sound better than it is. Then I feel bad about complaining. But this time I felt justified. "Yeah, well I might not be for much longer. Not after my TV disaster."

"A bit of bum flashing followed by a row is just an average night in Magaluf."

"Well, it wasn't Magaluf, it was national TV. So could you please stop turning everything into a joke?"

Kellie could tell I was serious. "Honestly, Rem, there's war, famine, global warming … *proper* serious issues out there, and if all the press can write about is your backside, *they're* the ones with a problem, not you."

"Yeah, s'pose so. Anyway… How's *Rebecca*?"

"Oh, she has definitely replaced you." Kellie started to giggle. (She knows me so well.)

"You cow."

Then she suddenly got serious. "Have you heard from James?"

I haven't spoken to my ex-BMF for seventeen long months. For the first couple of months I was still angry with him for denying his boyfriend had laced my drink; but for the past fifteen, I've missed him. BADLY.

"Nope. Why would I have heard from *him*?"

"Well, he said that he'd—"

"Hang on, have you spoken to him?"

"A couple of times," she mumbled.

"You traitor!"

"I'm not. And if you call him, you'll know why."

"No way am I calling him."

"Yeah, you'd much rather hang out with your Yankee granny friend."

She was talking about Suzy Raymond. According to Malibu and Kellie, Suzy isn't just square – she's judgemental and boring too. They have a bit of a point; both Raymonds think the British drink too much for a start. #fail

"Maybe I would. In fact, I owe her a call."

"You mean she's still talking to you after that tacky exposing of bum flesh? *Oh–h my–y goodness*," she said in Suzy's voice.

"Actually, she sent a nice text about it," I said defensively. OK, I know it was a bit cringe, but Kellie didn't need to know that.

"Did she? What did it say?"

I knew Kel would crack a joke about the "believe in your-self" part of Suzy's text so I only repeated, "Ish happens."

"'Ish'? What the hell's *ish*?"

"You know she doesn't swear."

She put on Suzy's voice again. "No. And she also poops roses."

"Yeah, right. Anyway, I think you should know… She has replaced you."

She cracked up. "Love you too. Always and for ever."

"Whatev'."

Twenty seconds after we rang off, @Kelz tweeted: *@RemyBennet is my wifey for life xxx*

So I tweeted back: *@Kelz cosign xx*

Then spent the rest of my lunch break searching every bit of my picture in the *Metro* for flaws. Apart from the obvious need for a firmer butt, I also need tighter arms and thinner thighs – basically I NEED LIPOSUCTION.

6.30 p.m.

Done my last customer for today. Charlie and Isabel are still busy, but when Lara's last appointment cancelled half an hour ago, I told her she could go home and I'd lock up. She deserves an early night. Took a while, but I happen to be in a v. good mood.

1. Because I'm going to see my man tonight.
2. Because I've had three texts complimenting my pic in the *Metro* – from Mum and Dad (will have

to take with a pinch of salt, as parents) but also from Blow-dry Sarah (who, for her sins, is still working at Kara's).

3. Because I've received twice as many complimentary tweets as insulting ones. Replied to as many as I could with *Thanks x* – after I'd shed a couple of tears over the insulting ones. Ugh! No matter how strong I tell myself to be, one or two always get to me first.

Don't want to hog the happiness bubble or anything but the day would be complete if James called to say that he'd seen the pic too. He always reads the *Metro*.

Before she left, Lara said I should consider opening a new salon because Tah-dah! was doing so well. Told her that the salon's success was due to how well she'd been running the place; and she said no, it'd been my idea to focus on nails, waxing and tanning – which she'd had her doubts about at the beginning – that had set my salon apart from everywhere else.

"Especially from Kara's. She must be gutted about the way things have turned out."

She's probably right. My old boss, Kara "Feminazi" Cooper, doesn't talk to me any more. She maintains it has nothing to do with loads of her customers switching over to Tah-dah!, and everything to do with me revealing that her nickname had been "the Feminazi" during an interview with the local paper.

"And let's face it, your profile hasn't hurt," added Lara.

Was she saying the success is mostly due to my "profile"? I wasn't sure, but as it's the nicest thing Lara has ever said about me (to my face at least), I thanked her.

"I'm serious. I reckon you could do the same again, no problem."

Another salon was always my original plan. I actually wanted a whole salon empire. But how can I open another one when I'm so bloody busy with this celebrity shizz?!

Thanks for all the compliments, guys. And all those being negative can do one! Today is a #trollfreezone

10.30 P.M.

Stephen was proper pale when he opened the door to me.

"You look like death," I told him.

"Ta. I love yer too."

I offered to make him something light to eat, but his best friend Angus – who is still living with him RENT-FREE – had made him some chicken noodle soup.

"Get this down yer, Stevie boy," he said. "Got the recipe from Gordon."

I took it that Angus meant Gordon Ramsay. He's never met him, or any other famous chef whose recipes he uses, but he always name-drops as if they're one of his best mates. "Chef" Angus has done loads of compensation cooking in this year of allegedly searching for work (sorry, but I have my suspicions) and his meals are always tasty. Must admit, the chicken noodle soup was delish. Stephen didn't eat a lot of it though. Poor thing. He's still feeling rough, and definitely should still be at home, but he's worried about missing training.

"I'm sure yer'll still make the first team. Yer scored a few in Japan," Angus reminded him. (He's the resident cheerleader too.)

"Aye. But not as many as *some* people..."

At this, Angus gave me evils as if it's my fault Stephen and Robbie play for the same team – another one of his "jobs": bodyguard of Stephen's emotions. He's well over the top when we're out – shoos people away from us, if he decides they've come too close. And don't dare make a snide remark. When we were clubbing at Whisky Mist a few months ago, Angus squared up to a weedy little bloke he'd overheard saying Stephen can't score goals. Ended up grabbing him by the shirt and lifting him off the floor. "Der yer wanna say that again, yer little prick?" he screamed in his face. Weedy Little Bloke complained to security and they came up to us ten minutes later, warning us to calm Angus down or they'd have to throw us out. So–o embarrassing!

I'm far from perfect, I know that, but I've gone over this a hundred times and this messed-up situation has everything to do with sheer bad luck and nothing to do with me. When I met Stephen I had no idea that he was a footballer, let alone that he was about to join my ex's team! Robbie and Stephen hate each other even more since they had the fight that launched my new career. They constantly try to outdo each other on the pitch, and I think their manager uses it to keep them both scoring goals. In interviews he says things like, "I think Robbie Wilkins will be my top scorer this season, but it's possible for Stephen Campbell to be a close second." That really gets Stephen going. And Angus. And the Campbell clan back in Scotland. Me too, of course, although not so much because, to be honest, I still don't get football. I just want Stephen to be happy.

He started to wilt about half an hour ago, and now he's asleep. I, on the other hand, am most definitely awake. Lara has sparked something in me and I can't stop thinking about what she said.

NEW SALON

Pros	Cons
I love the idea!	Won't have time to run it
	Expensive.
	Could lose all my savings
	(unless I find an investor).

OK, so this isn't ideal but I'm still buzzing about the idea. Also think I've solved one of the problems: *I* may not be able to run it, but Malibu can! And, seeing as she needs to get back on her feet, that kills two birds. Genius!

She'll really appreciate it too – relying on Gary for money must be half the reason she's down. He only pays basic maintenance for Gary Junior. Nothing compared with how much he earns. Mum told her to take him to court, but Mal said he'd only bring up how she cheated on him, and she doesn't want to wash her dirty knickers in public. Methinks it's actually because she wants to get back with Gary, but she needs to realize that might not happen. And when she does, she'll look for a back-up plan – aka ME. I'm even willing to make it a partnership; we can split the profits 50–50.

I've just sent her a text telling her to call me! #excitingtimes

10.50 P.M.

When Mal phoned I said, "I think I've found a way for us to work together again."

And she replied, "No way! So have I."

I couldn't believe it. I've read articles about sisters breaking their arm at the same time, or even giving birth on the same day – admittedly, they're usually twins – but could us Bennet sisters actually have thought up the same plan at the exact same moment?

NO.

"Go on then, what's yours?" she asked.

"Opening a new salon, with you running it!"

"Oh."

"Why, what were you thinking?"

"Something way better than that."

"Mal, I've really enjoyed running the salon. I think you'd enjoy it too."

"Yeah, but it's nothing compared with what you're doing now, is it? You're living the dream."

I sighed. "I suppose I am." While Kellie makes my situation sound better than it is, Malibu makes it sound like I've won the blooming lottery.

"*So*, I've been thinking. Now that you've gone viral and all that, it's time to take things to the next level. I'm talking about us becoming a British version of the Kardashians."

Pause.

"Have you had a drink?"

"No! Think about it, Rem – our own TV show! *Being the Bennets* – epic title, eh!"

She has clearly lost it. Why would anyone want to do a TV show about us? I'm a Z-lister; she's a Z-lister's sister!

"Look, we can always change the title if you don't like it. But our *own* show, Rem. It'll be brilliant! *And* it'll be a chance to show Gary that I don't need him."

Well, at least we were agreed on one thing, I thought.

"Phone that producer – let's sell it to him," she pressed.

"What producer?"

"The one who gave you his card the other night. The *Silver Fox*. He loved us."

"Did he?"

"Yeah. Of course he did."

"Er… Bit late now. Let's leave it till tomorrow."

Going to bed. My head hurts.

Saturday 3 August – 9.25 a.m.

Popping into the salon for a bit, after my personal training session with she-who-holds-no-hostages Mimi Taylor. Last time, I begged her for mercy so I could get out of doing my last set of sit-ups.

"I can't do any more; I'm dead," I said as I lay there like a sweaty corpse.

"You can't be dead – you're talking," she told me. "For that you can do an extra set."

Can't believe I'm actually pay for that shizz. But I have one more Terri Catalogue photo shoot to do before my contract's up, and if I don't look good they might not offer me another one.

When I'm finished in the salon later, I'm going to Scotland with Stephen. It's all a bit last-minute but Stephen reckons we might as well use his two days off to visit his family; and Lara said she'd be fine to run the salon without me (let's face it, that's actually what she's been doing all year).

Stephen's been a brilliant boyfriend and booked us an ace hotel in the Scottish Highlands, so we'll only spend a couple of hours in Glasgow with his family. He says he wants me to see the true beauty of Scotland. To be honest, that's the reason I agreed to go, as Glasgow's OK but I have an ickle problem with the Campbells: they hate me. I think they hated me before they even met me. I knew as soon as I was introduced to his mum and she shook my hand, then smiled as if she were constipated.

"Maybe it's because you're English," Dad said when I filled him in. "Historically, the Scots don't much like the English."

"Duh! I have seen *Braveheart*."

Kellie said it probably had nothing to do with me being English; more likely they thought I was a gold-digger – "Which you're not, of course," she added. "But so many of these WAGs are."

Yeah. Like Stephen's ex-girlfriend, Rosie.

Hmm. Will make sure I drop in how well the salon is doing. And that I'm getting paid a mint for my clothing range... Gold-digger my ass.

Hey @MimiFitness, I'm on my way. Go easy on me.
LOL! x

1.30 P.M.

Some things just don't go together: the two ends of a magnet; Rihanna + roll-necks; exercise + Remy Louise Bennet. Did so many squats my bum cheeks cramped. Walked into the salon like I'd soiled my pants.

Even worse news – Angus has decided to see his family in Glasgow too. Acting the true martyr, he said that he could only afford to take the bus, and when he added that it would take nine hours, Stephen said, "Dawn't be silly. I'll get yer a ticket so yer can fly with us."

This was no surprise to me – Angus is Stephen's man-child. What I didn't expect was that this meant we'd all be there in time to watch the charity football match Angus's sister was playing in, and that Angus would suggest we went with him. Stephen and Angie used to be an item. OK, they broke up when they were fifteen, but that doesn't give Stephen the right to look at me questioningly as if watching her play was an option. I made sure my eyes transmitted back: **not in this frickin' lifetime**.

He got the hint. "Thanks fer asking, Big Man, but we'll need to get to the hotel."

While Stephen was packing his last bits I finally phoned Suzy Raymond. She wanted me to know that she was in my corner, one hundred per cent.

"We all make mistakes, right?"

Yep. Some are bigger than others though, and I can't help thinking Suzy's biggest slip-up is probably forgetting to tip a cab driver. ☺

<u>Sunday 4 August – 10 a.m.</u>

Good morning tweeple. The Scottish Highlands are beautiful!

The hotel we're staying in is stunning. It's called the Highland Manor and the grounds stretch on for ever – lush greens as far as the eye can see, with a lake that guests can fish in. Our room has the type of four-poster bed and large stone fireplace that I reckon Henry the Eighth had back in the day. Outside, you inhale the air and know you're as far away from the pollution of London as you can possibly be. You feel revitalized and ready to go – I bet no one needs Red Bull up here. LOL! Anyhoo, I feel brand new – so new that I actually contemplated having a make-up-free Sunday, like the old days. I figured there'd be no paparazzi up here. Then I realized there'd probably be tons of hotel guests with camera phones – can't take any chances. ☹

Stephen's most definitely a new man today. This morning he felt good enough to go for a jog. He hasn't come back yet but when he does, we're going to have some breakfast and then watch films in bed. BLISS. ☺ ☺

More good news – methinks I've made a breakthrough with the Campbells! Once I'd swapped constipated smiles with his mum, she asked how I was. "Couldn't be better," I said. "The salon's always fully booked, and it looks like Terri Catalogue are about to renew my contract for a hu–uuuge wedge."

"Aw. That's good," Mrs Campbell replied. "But I was thinking more how yer doing personally – you know, since *Good Morning A.M.*"

Oops!

"Mum. I told yer not ter bring that up!" Stephen hissed as I went red.

"Aye, of course yer did. I forgot."

Mr Campbell came to the rescue. "Anyone want a cup of tea?"

We all said yes and when Mrs Campbell offered to make it, I followed her through to the kitchen to help.

"I really am sorry about that," she said as she took the cups out. "Me and my big mouth!"

"It's OK. But as you can imagine, I'm majorly embarrassed about it," I admitted.

"Aye, I can see that. Still, it was good ter see someone give it ter that Lorraine Edinbugger Macintosh." She suddenly graced me with her first genuine smile. ☺

10.20 a.m.

Was standing in front of the mirror, squeezing my thighs to see what they'd look like if they were thin, when Malibu phoned.

"Have you called him yet?" she asked.

"Called who?" I said, confused.

"The *Silver Fox!*"

"Oh, *him*. No, sorry – forgot."

"How can you forget such a big thing? Go on, call him. *Now*. We need to strike while the iron's hot."

"*On a Sunday*. Even Him upstairs took a break on Sundays."

"Just ca–aall."

I thought about getting real with her by pointing out the Z-ness of our celebrity status, but that might have been too blunt. (As Mum said, I have to "choose my words carefully".) Instead I said, "To be honest, Mal, I don't think a programme on us two will work."

"Why?"

"Because … I don't."

"All right, if you wanna be like that," she said in a huff. Then she cut me off. ☹

‖ P.M.

Just got home and it looks like everyone's in bed.

Today was amazing. When he got back from his jog, Stephen climbed into bed and we snuggled and kissed for ages. *We could do this all the time if we lived together,* I thought.

"Rem?" he said suddenly.

"Yeah?"

"Yer didn't tell me Terri Catalogue renewed yer contract."

"Well, they haven't yet, but if this new PR woman does her job right, they should."

"Oh. And that's a good thing, then … yeah?"

"Well, it'll make me some good money."

"Aw, right."

"What's the matter?" I could tell something was wrong.

"Nothing. It's just … well … if yer going to keep up this celebrity thing, could yer please not talk about me in interviews?"

"Stephen, you're my boyfriend – you're bound to come up."

"Aye, I know, but this is a make-or-break season fer me and I need to concentrate on my game. When yer talk about me, the sports press start looking at me as a wannabe celeb instead of a proper sportsman. Then they're even more critical."

"Ugh!" It sounded like a big pile of BS to me. "Bet you wouldn't have said that to *Rosie*."

It took a while for him to open up about her, but Stephen eventually admitted that his experience with his ex-girlfriend was the reason he'd kept quiet about being a footballer when we first met. She was a model who broke his heart by leaving him for a millionaire when it looked like his football career had stalled – aka a professional gold-digger.

"Why've yer got to bring her up?"

"Because it's true."

"Of course it isn't. Look, babe, I've discussed it with Harry and he agrees."

"Well, Harry hasn't discussed it with *me*," I snapped.

"He should've done, then." Stephen named a few sportsmen who had seen their career nosedive since dating famous women. One of them was a rugby player called Toby Norton.

"He should consider himself lucky, cos I hadn't even heard of him until he started going out with *her.*"

"Well, ask Toby how *he* would've preferred yer to have heard of him." He cuddled me tighter and started to peck my neck. "I don't want us to fall out about this, OK?"

I sighed. "OK." But I was still in a right mood until he announced he'd booked me a treatment in the spa – a hot stone massage. Always wanted one of those. *You're forgiven,* I thought … *by about fifty-nine per cent.*

Gave Kel a quick call on my way down to the spa.

"He's ashamed of me, I know he is. He's probably heard all the Bumquake jokes and I'll be dumped by next week."

"Don't be ridic'. He wouldn't spend a fortune taking you away if he was about to dump you. Though even if he did, you'd have no problems pulling someone else. Everyone with an Internet connection has seen you don't wear knickers."

"I *do*. It was a thong."

Sometimes, when Kel jokes about my problems, I start to pine for James. ☹

The spa had super-stylish black tiled walls. Pan-pipe music drifted out of invisible speakers; the smell of scented candles filled the room; and a large water feature met you as soon as you came through the door. If peace were a place, I had just walked into it. The woman who did my massage, Amanda, had a lovely soothing voice: "Let me know if you need less or more pressure," she said. "Apart from that, close your eyes and enjoy."

I more than enjoyed. Each time she kneaded a knot in my back, she squashed out of me any thought of being dumped; and once I was relaxed, I went into a dream-state... Stephen was asking me to live with him... To marry him... To have his babies... Perfecto. ☺

Once the massage was over, I asked Amanda to point out the salon's manager so I could sing her praises officially.

She was really chuffed. "Though technically, we don't have a salon manager," she explained. "She went off to have a baby but she's just decided she's not coming back."

"Well, you were brilliant today," I told her, and made myself a mental note to tip her when we left.

Stephen had gone for a sports massage and he was back in the room five minutes after me.

"How was it?"

"Loved it. Thanks, baby," I said. *And I love* you, I thought. ☺

11.30 p.m.

Aa–aaargh! Nightmare. Mum was listening out for me; she just came in for a "little chat".

"I hear you and Malibu had an argument."

"I didn't argue with her. I simply pointed out a fact, then *she* cut me off."

"Well, she's been crying this evening."

"It can't be because of me. Must be something to do with Gary."

Mum shook her head. "You're living her dream, Remy – have you ever stopped to consider that?"

No, I hadn't. And I suppose it must be hard. But no harder than me spending nineteen years of my life putting up with people gasping over how beautiful *she* is.

"It's not my fault this has happened to me," I said after a while.

"I know. And she's happy for you, but it doesn't make it any easier. If there's any way you can help her; any way at all…"

I sighed. "OK, Mum. I get it. I'll phone the TV producer."

Monday 5 August – 8 a.m.

Had a little lapse in the Highlands so … I am Remy Louise Bennet. I am not perfect. But I still love—

8.15 a.m.

Just got interrupted by Malibu knocking on my door. She's been behaving like an over-enthusiastic puppy ever since.

"Mum said you're gonna phone the Silver Fox. Yay! Sorry about yesterday, by the way – was probably a bit stroppy!"

D'ya think?!

"*Anyways*, we're about to be ridiculously famous! I just know it."

"Uh-huh."

"The Kardashians made sixty million last year. SIXTY MILLION. So you'd better work out how you're going to spend the money."

"Yeah." *roll eyes*

"Come on, let's phone him now."

I could only humour her so much. "It's too early."

"He'll be up. We're up, aren't we? Phone him."

"Um… Where's my lovely nephew?"

"Mum's giving him breakfast. Come on, Silver Fox time, *now*."

"Wait a minute, Mal. *Wait*… Breathe."

"Am I talking fast?"

"Very."

She inhaled… "Right. Call him."

"Maybe we should run through what to say first."

She thought about it. "OK. Good point," she admitted. Phew!

"I'll show you my business plan," she said.

WTF?!

She'd covered three sides of A4 with her business plan to turn us into the Kardashians. She never submitted that much in two years of GCSE English coursework! Along with the TV show, she's given us a brand name – M 'n' R – and products: make-up, bags and perfume.

"What d'you think?"

"It's very …" – was actually thinking "deluded" but chose my words carefully – "… *ambitious*."

"That's a good thing, though, right?"

"Er… Yeah."

"We want him to see that we're aiming high. The Kardashians are switched on – their mum knows how to print money."

"Right."

"Go on then, call!"

She was actually standing right behind me, breathing down my neck as I held the business card and dialled the number for the TV producer Robert Fitzgerald.

Got his voicemail. Phew! Couldn't end the call quick enough.

"You should've left a message," she moaned. "Why didn't you leave a message?"

Decided to introduce a tiny bit of reality. "Mal, he might not even remember us."

"Course he will. He thought we were great. Pass me the phone."

I gave it to her and she pressed redial. Voicemail. *Beep!*

"Hey Robert, it's Malibu Bennet. You met me and my sister *Remy Bennet* at the charity do the other night. You liked our Nancy Scott dresses. But you'll probably remember Remy at any rate – she's the one who *flashed her bum* on *Good Morning A.M.*"

Grrrr.

"Anyway," she continued, "we have a great idea for a TV show. It's going to be bigger than the Kardashians and I think you'll be interested, so give us a call."

Mal reeled off my number, ended the call and then said, "Trust me. It's in the bag!"

She's clueless. But I have bigger problems to deal with, like a boyfriend who won't let me speak about him in public!

8.50 a.m.

Called Harry.

"Stephen doesn't want me to talk about him in interviews."

"Yeah, he did mention somefin' like that. I was about to call. Your *Here* mag article's bin sent to me. It's coming out tomorrow."

"And?"

"I'm 'aving a conference call with Camilla Douglas-Smith. Think it'll be best if we all talk about it together. Can you come in for ten-thirty?"

"All right then," I said, although I was meant to go into the salon this morning. Will go in after my session with Dr Clein instead.

9.05 a.m.

Robert "Silver Fox" Fitzgerald just rang!

"Remy Bennet," he sang, "how are you, darling?"

Wow, he was chirpy. "Me? Yeah… I'm good."

"Great. We wondered where you got to the other

night – one minute you were going to the loos, the next you'd disappeared."

"Yeah, erm, Malibu had had a few too many and she felt really sick," I pretended (about her feeling sick, anyway).

"Oh. Well, I just got her message about you having an idea that's, and I quote, 'bigger than the Kardashians'."

"Malibu thinks so, anyway."

"I'm all ears."

"Um… Can you hold a second, please?" Opened my bedroom door. "Malibu!" At least if she explained it, he'd know I wasn't the one stupid enough to think we're superstars in the making.

"What d'you want?" she snapped from her room next door.

"Robert Fitzgerald's on the phone."

Malibu materialized within seconds and grabbed the phone out of my hand.

"Hiya Robert. Hope I wasn't too tipsy the other night? Good. Listen, I could tell you a bit about it now but I think it'd be much better for us to meet up."

I started to shake my head.

But Malibu looked at me and nodded. "You're the first person we've called but obviously we'll have to speak to other TV producers… Yeah, yeah, Wednesday sounds good. Shall we say eleven? Perfect. See you then." ☺

9.35 a.m.

Suddenly realized how late I was running. Showered and dressed quicker than the speed of light. In cab now. Dying to see *Here* mag.

> So wish I was back at Highland Manor. Best hot stone massage ever! #withdrawalsymptoms

7.50 p.m.

Found out some interesting things during the conference call with Camilla:

1. PR stands for public relations.
2. PR people give information to the press to publicize their client in the best possible light – and to hell with everyone else, even boyfriends!
3. There's actually someone way bossier than Malibu: Camilla Douglas-Smith.

The *Here* mag article had a full-page pic of me in the beautiful wedding dress, with the headline **"I've already picked our kids' names"**.

Yikes!

"Does that make me sound desperate?"

"Well, have you?" asked Harry.

"Um, maybe."

"Well then, yes."

"Wrong, Harry!" Camilla snapped through the

loudspeaker. "All girls have done it. And now they'll know you're exactly the same as them, instead of believing that your footballer boyfriend, clothing range, et cetera means you could never be their friend. And women being able to relate to you is a very lucrative prospect. This isn't just a rebranding, dahling, this is you moving forward."

I quickly scanned the article. Sam for Short had written gushing comments about Stephen: *He is the "Braveheart" who sprang to defend Remy's honour on the pitch in one of the most romantic moments of last year.* However, there was a "but": *Which begs the question why he hasn't proposed. "He hasn't even asked me to live with him!"* she quoted me as saying.

"Hmm. Does that proposal bit make me sound desperate?"

"In a word, yes," answered Harry.

"Wrong again, Harry," Camilla chimed in. "Thousands of women are hanging on for a proposal *right now*. And being someone people can relate to is—"

"A very lucrative prospect – *we heard*. But I 'appen to have a client who only wants to be spoken about in the press if it's something to do with football."

"Then perhaps you shouldn't be representing both of them, Harry. Because I assure you that Remy speaking about her ups and downs with Stephen will sway people's opinions about her. And *she's* who *I* am working for."

"Looking after both of them isn't ideal, I admit. But Remy," Harry said, looking me straight in the eye, "Stephen won't like it. I promise ya."

"Remy, I'm moments away from booking you on *Life*

Stories. If it goes well, it could change your career *for ever*. So, excuse my French here, Stephen will have to grow some balls."

Aa–aaaaaaaargh!

Stormed into Dr Clein's office and spilled my guts. "Just fed up with everyone bossing me around!"

"Well, why don't you try doing what *you* want to do?" he asked.

"Because… It's not as simple as that."

"Isn't it?"

"Apparently not. Not if I want a career."

"A salon career?"

"No. In TV and stuff. I mean *Life Stories* is massive. Me and Mal always watch it, and have a good cry."

"How do you think Stephen will react if you talk about him on the show?"

I sighed because there was no need to "think" – I KNEW. "I'll cross that bridge when I come to it."

"Remy, if this TV career is important enough for you to risk your relationship with Stephen, why are you so bothered about Malibu pushing for your own show – surely that's a good thing?"

"Well, on paper maybe. But it just doesn't feel right."

Dr Clein thought for a second. "Do you like being famous?"

"Um… S'pose so. Everyone wants to be famous, don't they?"

"Do they?"

And that's when the session ended.

I then headed over to the salon and immediately felt better. Apart from the odd customer intent on beating up a mistress, everyone there just wants to have a trouble-free day. They're the kind of people I want to surround myself with. Debbie Wyatt has only gone and got herself a toyboy – ALREADY. She passed by the salon to show him off. Said she met him in a pub two days ago and he hasn't left her side since. ☺

Lara said, "Good for you Debbie," and gave her a high-five.

It took a while but I really like Lara now. So far she's the only person to ask how my Scotland trip went. Told her how excellent it was and about my to-die-for hot stone massage. As usual, I reported back on the competition:

"Their salon looked the part, had top-of-the-range products, and the lady who did my massage was top-drawer."

Lara looked a bit wounded.

"But she's not *salon manager* material – definitely couldn't run the place like you do."

On the way home I thought, *OK, I'm not one hundred per cent sure why I'm not jumping up and down about this TV show with Mal (IF Robert Fitzgerald is dumb enough to give us one). But I'm going to that meeting on Wednesday and will do my best to get it made. And it won't be any old TV show either. This one will make Kim Kardashian and her sisters kiss our perfectly pedicured Bennet feet!* #bowdownbiatches

Spent the night at Stephen's. Felt guilty as soon as he opened the door to me, and before I knew it I was grassing myself up.

"Baby, I know I agreed not to talk about you in interviews but there's one coming out tomorrow that I did when you were in Japan. In *Here* mag."

"Aw." He looked disappointed. "What yer saying?"

"Good things. I promise you."

"Like?"

I pictured myself in the wedding dress, then the "kids' names" headline, and quietly died inside. *Here* mag might as well have written DESPERATE across my forehead.

"Oh, just girly stuff. Boring really." It's one thing looking desperate in a magazine, but another admitting it to the man who hasn't even asked you to live with him yet. Would have preferred to boil a bunny!

"No more now though. OK?"

"OK," I said. And I'm not proud of it, but I crossed my fingers just in case *Life Stories* comes off.

Home now, and dressed for training. Have a session with Mimi later. First, want to get Mal's view on the *Here* mag article.

11.55 a.m.

"Did you actually admit that you'd picked kids' names or

73

was the journalist making that up?" asked Malibu when she'd read the whole thing.

"No, that was me."

"Well, you probably should buy a flat. He's going to run a mile."

Aa–aaaaaaargh!

"The dress *is* beautiful though."

"Every cloud…" I groaned.

"You never know, I could be wrong and it'll push him into proper commitment."

"What do your guts say?" I asked tentatively.

"Buy a flat."

Why am I such an idiot?

"Don't worry about it for now. We've got far more important things to talk about." Malibu meant our meeting with Robert Fitzgerald tomorrow of course. She had it all planned out.

"I'll be the good cop, you're going to act the bad cop," she said.

"Act? I can't act. And why've I got to be the baddie, anyway?"

"Cos you're a celebrity – you can get away with being a stroppy diva. And the way I wanna play it, Robert will be lapping up whatever I say while you're acting like you don't want to do it. Before you know it, he'll be convincing *you* to do the show instead of us trying to convince him. Classic Jedi mind trick."

"How d'you think this stuff up, Mal?"

"When you've got a mouth to feed, you think up a lot of stuff."

I asked her how it was going with Gary and she sighed.

"He's not sure whether he can forgive me one hundred per cent for the Lance thing. I said I'd take fifty per cent, but he says it has to be a hundred. Well, that's not gonna happen."

"Don't worry. Once this TV show comes off, he'll be begging you to get back with him," I told her.

"Yeah. But I might have nabbed myself a Grammy-winning rapper by then." She smiled but I know she didn't mean it. She's crazy about Gary.

I showed Mum *Here* mag to get a second opinion. She took one look at the headline and said, "You're pregnant? That's no way to break it to your mother."

"No, Mum, I've picked kids' names for when I *do* start having babies."

"Oh."

"What d'you think?"

"Well… We used to choose baby names when we were young too," she said, as if she were ancient. "But in *my* time, girls kept that to themselves. Admitting something like that would have given a man cold feet."

Oh Lawd. ☺

2 P.M.

To everyone wishing congrats. Cheers but not preggers.
Bit of a confusing headline. :-) #HereMag

OMG just been killed by @MimiFitness! Had aching quads and six missed calls by the time she'd finished with me. Five of them were from Stephen. Knew that probably meant I was in deep poo. Still, played it cool when I returned his call, just in case. "Hi baby," I chirped when he answered.

"What are yer playing at?" he growled back. Holy crap! He'd seen the article then.

"Moi?" I said innocently.

"I resent yer portraying me as a bad guy because we don't live together when *yer* the one looking for yer own flat!"

"It wasn't like that, babe! She asked whether marriage was on the cards so all I said was we're taking one step at a time, seeing as we don't even live together. It's been twisted into something else by *her!*"

"Stitched up by a journalist? Easy way out."

"I'm serious! Why would I say something that would put you off wanting to marry me?"

Those last two words seemed to hang in the air as if I'd said them inside a very large cave.

Oh–hhh shit.

"Not that I think you're considering marriage or anything," I said quickly, "but … well … I… You know what I mean."

"Naw, I don't. Explain."

Now I know the real meaning of awkward. "Well, I mean that if… Well, if I thought you were ever thinking

76

of … asking me something that could possibly lead to a … a … thingy … then I wouldn't have my pictures taken in a wedding dress and talk about picking kids' names. I mean, *as if*! That would obviously make you run a mile. Der!"

There was a pause.

"Aye. Yer a lotta things, Remy, but stupid isn't one of them," he said, sounding more like the Stephen I love. Phew!

"Thanks. Look, I'm sorry. It sucks and I hate it, and I told people it's a load of crap on Twitter. I can write an even stronger tweet now if you like?"

"Naw, don't bother. That'll only spark more talk about it, and I told yer – I want people to concentrate on my football this season, not gossip about my private life."

He's lucky he's got football because when it comes to me, my private life/mental state is all anyone seems to be interested in. Even after I shared personal stuff for this blooming *Here* mag interview, Sam for Short still didn't print any of the stuff I'd said about running a salon.

"Look, I knaw it's my fault for fighting that day but I need to move on. Every time it comes up in the press, things get said in training and…" He trailed off. It must be hard to be in the same team as Robbie twot-face. And he's put up with it for a whole eighteen months. "No more talk about us – OK? I really mean it."

"I promise," I said, and this time I didn't cross my fingers. "How did you find out about it, anyway? Didn't have you down as a *Here* mag kind of guy."

"My mum. She read the headline and thought I was making her a grandma."

"Oh shit. I'm sorry."

Typical. Decided to call straight away and explain.

"It was amazing how quickly I warmed to the idea," Stephen's mum said. "I actually pictured a wee bairn."

"These journalists, you know, they just get so ahead of themselves."

"Aye, I see that. But I did like those Scottish baby names. Very grand."

"Aye," I replied. WTF?!

The other missed call had been from Robert Fitzgerald, and he'd left a message: "Fantastic article in *Here* mag, darling! *Loved* it. See you soon."

3 P.M.

Malibu's been banging on about the meeting tomorrow. I really wasn't in the mood.

But a call from Lara has cheered me up. She's heard about a salon she thinks I'd love to take over. Her friend works there, but the boss is closing it down because the landlord has almost doubled the rent. He's willing to sell if someone prefers buying to renting, and the salon comes with a one-bedroomed flat above it. Woo-hoo!!!

"Where is it?" I asked.

"A couple of streets away from Selfridges."

Wow. A proper classy location. People are loaded

around there. Lara must think I'm made of money.

That's another thing about this celebrity malarkey – everyone assumes you're rolling in it. OK, the Terri Catalogue deal means I have the deposit for a flat saved up, but apart from that, as the cash comes in, the cash flies out – and I'm talking super-fast. Mostly it goes on things that didn't figure in my life before – I'm paying for a psych and a frickin' PR woman who patronizes me to death, for a start! On top of that, I have to buy way more clothes than I used to. I can't be pictured in the same thing twice. Plus the clothes have to be designer and on-trend – the fashion columns are crueller than any Netherfield Park WAG.

Anyhoo, Lara gave me the address and I said I'd have a look before I pop into Tah-dah!

8 P.M.

Visited the potential new salon. Was v. impressed with the location, and the flat was gorgeous. Thought it had my name on it until the landlord told me the price: sixty-five grand a year to rent the salon and flat; five hundred thousand to buy! What a joke. That's way out of my league. Just finished having a right old rant about it to Stephen.

"Didn't realize you wanted to open another salon," he said. "Yer barely have time for the one you've got now."

"I'd get someone else to run it," I explained.

"Oh. So you intend to keep up this celebrity thing then?"

"Well… I reckon I should. I mean, I've been lucky enough to get it, haven't I?"

"That's one way of looking at it, I suppose."

"What's the matter?" I could tell something was on his mind.

"I'll tell yer when I see yer. What yer doing tomorrow?"

"A meeting in the morning. Otherwise, I'd be with you right now."

"With the catalogue?"

"Er … no. Something boring. I won't even waste your time." This wasn't the time to tell him about a Bennet sisters TV show that probably wasn't going to happen anyway. Decided to change the subject, pronto. "Wow, the season starts next Saturday – bet you can't wait!"

"Yeah. S'pose so."

Then I phoned Dad and complained about the price of the potential new salon.

"It is in a prime location though," he said.

"That's true. So would you be interested in investing again, seeing as Tah-dah! has worked out so well?"

"I'm not made of money, love. Have you thought about asking Stephen? Because if you guys are thinking of settling down, it'll be a good way to work together. That's all marriage is, you know – *teamwork*."

Dad had clearly been reading *Here* mag.

"Dad, that article was a load of balls."

"Really?"

"Yes. *But talking of settling down*, how's it going with

Elizabeth? Made a decision yet? You can't keep a good woman waiting too long."

I like Elizabeth. She's massively improved Dad's dress sense and keeps him in check without being a ball-breaker.

"Have you, um ... spoken to your mum?"

"What about?"

He sighed. "She sent me some divorce papers. So I suppose that's it. Final."

"Sorry, Dad, I didn't realize."

"Anyway, with that to deal with on top of the business with your Uncle Pete, I'm not sure I'd have the head space to take on another salon."

"Bloody Mum," I muttered.

"She's moved on, Remy. You can't blame her for that."

Dad's right. Mum chose Alan a long time ago and he seems to be here for good – Dad's so blooming forgiving. Malibu would probably give up fake tan to have her Gary be like that.

9 P.M.

Mal turned my bedroom into a catwalk earlier. She modelled a ridiculous amount of outfits for the meeting tomorrow. They were all tight or short or both. Once she'd decided what to wear – the floral print playsuit – I said, "Mum's sent Dad some divorce papers."

And she said, "Yeah, I know."

Humph! Why am I always the last to know what's going on in this house?!

<u>Wednesday 7 August - 8.45 a.m.</u>

I am Remy Louise Bennet. I am not perfect. But I still love being me.

Malibu has already been in to go over the plan. She means business. Gary phoned in the middle of her briefing and she didn't even answer his call!

<u>1 p.m.</u>

He–eelp! Think I need a doctor. Actually thought I was having a heart attack this morning!!

It began just before the meeting with Robert Fitzgerald. On the way to his office, Malibu said, "Please don't let me down, Rem. This idea is the only thing I've got."

"What about Gary Junior?"

She glared at me. "You know what I mean."

I promised I'd do my best, but when she knocked on his office door, my heart rate suddenly went ballistic and I got a strange pain in my chest. WTF?!

"Come in," Robert Fitzgerald called out.

I took a long, deep breath as I followed Malibu into the room, then another one as we sat on the posh leather sofa facing him. The chest pain had died down but my heart rate was still all over the place, and when I tried to take deep breaths it felt like all the oxygen had been sucked out of the room.

"Girls, great to see you again," Robert said. He looked friendly enough, with his big gleaming, bright white smile. "How are you?"

"May I use your loo?" I blurted out.

When I got there, I bent over the sink and splashed my face with cold water. Then spent the next ten minutes slow-breathing like a yoga pro. Eventually, my heart rate came down to normal-ish. Decent enough to go back into the meeting, anyway. Phew!

Robert and Mal were finishing some small talk about the weather when I stepped back in.

"All we're asking for is a decent summer," said Mal as I rejoined her on the leather sofa.

"You all right?" she asked.

I nodded.

"Thought you'd disappeared again," joked Robert, and then he became all businesslike. "So, tell me about this TV show."

He'd met his match in Malibu. "Well, Rob, I've identified a gap in the market for a British show based on glamorous sisters like the Kardashians. And I think we're the ones for the job. We've got the looks, Remy's gone viral, and we're not short on personality either." She sounded even better than when she'd practised in my bedroom. She was giving a proper good account of herself, and I was actually beginning to feel a bit proud, when she started to add new stuff to her rehearsal spiel. "I'm the bubbly one. Remy, of course, is *Miss Controversy*. But what you may not be aware of, Rob, is our trump card: we both happen to be seeing Premiership footballers."

WTF?!

Robert's eyes lit up. "Well, obviously I saw your article in *Here* mag, Remy. But I had no idea about your situation, Malibu."

"Of course not – why would you? *I'm* not the celebrity. But you should know that both of our *Premiership footballers* would be well up for being in the show, wouldn't they, Rem?"

"Um... Well... Maybe we should..."

"It would be perfect if they were," Robert enthused. "That would make it a sure winner for ITV2."

"Amazing," said Malibu.

Remy Louise Bennet's Bitch Disclaimer

Now, let's make this clear. I am NOT a bitch. In fact, if anything, I reckon most people would describe me as kind and loyal. But I wasn't about to let my sister offer up my boyfriend for a TV show that there's no way he'd take part in. Especially when Robert Fitzgerald looked like he was falling in love with the idea. I had to do something to stop her. So I turned to Malibu and said, "You're not actually with Gary any more though, are you?"

OK, I admit it sounded a teensy-weensy bit bitchy, but

sounding like a bitch does not mean that you are one. Fact.

"Well, it's complicated," she said to me through gritted teeth. Then she forced a laugh. "You know how these things are, Rob. But I've got a son with him – Gary Johnson Junior – and, to be honest, it's been a proper dramatic journey. You never know, I might even confess all on the show."

She looked well pleased with herself. OMG! Was she being serious?

"Malibu, you can't go washing your dirty knickers in public – *remember*," I hissed.

"He wants me back, too," she continued. "*Badly.* I bet people would love to find out whether we actually kiss and make up."

What!!

"Don't be ridiculous!"

"I'm *not*!" She glared at me.

There was only one way to make her stop. "If you talk about what happened with Lance, Gary won't want anything to do with you."

Silence.

"Wow! This is great TV already." Robert laughed. "I'll call ITV and set up a meeting."

Then my heart rate went nuts again. I clutched my chest.

"Are you OK?"

"I ... just need some fresh air," I told them.

I walked out of the room as calmly as I could, then as soon as I'd shut the door behind me I bolted outside and stood on the pavement gasping for ages. Deep, deep breaths. Deeper, deeper breaths…

The feeling had worn off by the time Malibu came out, and I thought I'd sound like an idiot if I told her about it. Besides, she looked the happiest I've seen her in yonks. She held up her hand for a high-five. "Remy Bennet, you are the best actress England has ever produced," she said.

4 p.m.

Just got to the salon. Had an argument with Mum before I left. She's redecorating the front room AGAIN. This time she's channelling her obsession with *Downton Abbey* and going for a period feel, which involves covering the walls in (imitation) gold leaf. She had a massive tin of it in her hands. All I said was, "Mum, that doesn't exactly go with the Seventies curtains, does it?" and she said that I'm missing a sensitivity chip.

"*I'm* insensitive?! I'm not the one who sent her husband divorce papers and couldn't even be bothered to tell her own daughter!" Then I stomped off to my room before she could answer.

Ten minutes later Camilla Douglas-Smith called, saying she wants me to have interview technique lessons to prepare for *Life Stories*.

"Oh, so I'm definitely doing it?"

"A confirmation is imminent, dahling. And you need to be prepared. I've already established the narrative."

Eh?! Turns out that "narrative" means the storyline (in

a roundabout way) and this is mine, according to Camilla: "You are a girl from a council estate who has had fame thrust upon you because of circumstances beyond your control. You couldn't cope. No one in that position could. So, of cawse, on that fateful day on *Good Morning A.M.* you reacted like … well … any person from *your* background would."

"But I'm not from a council estate."

"Well, in my opinion, nor did the earth shake when you fell and flashed your bottom. Now, which one would you prefer people to believe?"

Aa–aaaaaargh! She's so blooming patronizing. Probably never met someone from a council estate, yet here she is, trying to make out that people who live on one are all troubled. Wanted to bin her there and then, but as I've already paid for her services, I said, *I'll be back* in my head – *Terminator* style. And believe me, I'm going to plan every single detail of her sacking.

As for potential heart attack… No sign. My heartbeat is so normal I'm wondering whether I made it all up.

Hey tweeple! Enjoy every day because you don't know if you'll be here tomorrow. #YOLO

7.10 P.M.

Salon's closed. Now waiting for Stephen. He's taking me out for dinner. ☺

When he said he had something to tell me face-to-face, I thought *Uh-oh*. But it can't be anything bad – not when he's booked a table at Simone's!!!! Simone's isn't any old restaurant, it's the place to be. Mal's been going on about it for ages. Checked it out online and it's only considered to be *the* most romantic restaurant in London. Woo-hoo!

The salon was huge on gossip this afternoon. The ~~best~~ major bit of info was that Lance Wilson has postponed his wedding to Amy Fitzgerald AGAIN. It's the third time now but this one was proper lastminute.com – the invites had been sent out and everything. Apparently he doesn't feel ready. Who would ever have guessed? *roll eyes*

Had to call Malibu to tell her the ~~good~~ news. "Thank God he didn't turn out to be Junior's father," she replied.

My "flirtation with death" this morning must have changed me because I genuinely felt sorry for Amy. She's always going on about marrying Lance. How humiliating. The girls in the salon didn't think she deserved any sympathy though – and neither did Malibu. "She made her bed, and she has my blessing to bloody well lie in it. Just like I had to."

Doh! Malibu and Gary's wedding was cancelled too. By Gary. Straight after she fessed up about her affair with Lance.

"Right. But I still don't think you should say stuff like that. It's bad for your karma."

"So I'll come back as a snake or something. So bloody what – it's worth it to see the smile wiped off Amy's smug face!"

Methinks Mal may be missing a sensitivity chip too. (Maybe it's a Bennet thing.)

Anyhoo, the good news is that I am now ninety-nine per cent positive that I'm not going to die. I Googled my symptoms on the way to the salon and it looks like I had a panic attack. Malibu still thinks I was acting. Said my performance at the meeting was Oscar-winning and she was gutted when I said I wasn't going home tonight, because she'd bought me a little present.

"You truly outfoxed the Silver Fox," she said. "Where're you guys going, anyway?"

Didn't want to sound too much of a show-off. "Oh … just Simone's."

"Simone's!" she exclaimed. "Lucky you – it's the most romantic restaurant in London. Oh–hhhh! I know what that means!"

"What?"

"I was wrong! That *Here* mag interview *has* kicked Stephen up the bum. He's gonna ask you to move in with him!"

"No way!"

"Of course. In fact, he might even go one better and propose."

"Don't be stupid!" I scoffed, although a part of me thought *Maybe!*

"Trust me."

Right, Remy, calm down. Do not set your hopes too high. It could be nothing.

Nothing at all. *sigh*

DISASTROUS NIGHT.

I'd worked myself up into a frenzy by the time we were seated at our table in Simone's. I'd convinced myself that he was going to propose. On the way there I'd gone through a range of questions in my head. Started with sensible ones: Do I want to get married? Am I too young? Hmm… Maybe we could have a long engagement? But before I knew it, questions had evolved into actual decisions: Right, Nancy Scott will make the wedding dress, Kellie and Mal will be my bridesmaids, and there will be lilies at the reception. No, not lilies – white roses. Yeah, roses – perfecto! It carried on as we waited for our meal to arrive. Then Stephen put his hand on my knee. It made me go all tingly, *This is IT*, I thought.

"Rem?"

"Yes, baby?"

"I've been thinking…"

"Uh-huh?"

"I don't think I'm going to be a regular starter for Netherfield Park so…"

Hmm. Bit of a strange start. Slow build. He's going for a slow build.

"… how would yer feel if I had the opportunity ter transfer to another team?"

"Another team?"

"Yes."

"Which team?"

"Um, Celtic."

"But aren't Celtic in … Scotland?"

Not big on football but even I knew that.

"Yes. Glasgow, ter be precise," said Stephen cautiously.

"Oh God, why Glasgow?"

"Cos it's my home."

I suppose there was that little detail.

"And I'm not going ter be happy sitting on the bench," he went on. "I need to be playing."

"But you probably will be. You were banging in the goals in Japan."

"Things change quickly in football, gorgeous. Harry says Celtic are willing to take me and they're promising that I'll start."

"Oh."

No marriage proposal, and now we were talking long-distance relationships. ☹

"And the thing is, Remy, I'd really like you ter…" He paused. "Well… I'd really like yer to come with me."

"Me? Live in Scotland?"

"Aye."

"With you?"

"Naw, Simon Cowell – *of course me*."

I should've been glad. He'd finally asked me to live with him, but after all my fantasizing it had lost its shine. And SCOTLAND!

"Well… It's so *unexpected*, I don't know what to say."

"I knaw it's happening a bit fast but we could get a place near the Highland Manor. Yer loved it there, didn't yer? And it's only forty minutes from the stadium."

Now I understood why he'd made such a big effort on his two days off. "Is that why you took me there? So you could talk me into living a gazillion miles away from my family?"

"I'm living away from *my* family now, don't forget."

"But that's part of your job. You're used to it."

"Naw, I'm not. This is the first time I've played outside Scotland."

"Yeah, but you've been doing it for nearly two years."

"It doesn't mean that I don't miss it. Because I do." I could see from his eyes that he was telling the truth. I've heard Stephen and Angus reminisce about things "back home", but I didn't realize that he would actually prefer to be there instead of London.

The waiter came and laid down two plates display-ing edible works of art. But Stephen and I barely touched anything.

I love him and I want to be with him, but moving to Scotland is major. I think he could see the doubt on my face.

"Look, it's worth being away from home if I'm playing but if I'm not… I'll just be miserable."

"But what if living in Scotland makes *me* miserable?"

Stephen sighed and held my hand tightly across the table. "I don't have all the answers, Rem. I just knaw how

92

I feel. Just say you'll think about it, OK? If things go to plan I'll be able to make the transfer deadline at the end of August."

"That's only three weeks away! You can't honestly expect me to make such a big decision in that time."

He sighed again. "That's football, babe."

"Yes, but you chose football – I *didn't*."

He said it's the kind of decision footballers' partners have to make all the time. Then he asked for the bill, paid, and we left. On the way back to his house I was thinking so hard about what to do that my brain hurt. Nothing seemed to make me want to live in Scotland though.

"What about the salon?" I said suddenly as Stephen was putting his key into the front door.

"What about it? Yer hardly there nowadays."

"That's right, dismiss the salon like it's nothing. Obviously chasing a leather ball is so–oo much more important than what I do."

"I respect what you've done with the salon, you know I do. But what I cannae respect is this celebrity crap. I don't know why yer want it so badly."

"It's not that I want it. It's just that it's happened and—"

"Because of me," he interrupted. "Don't yer forget that."

"Oh yeah, it's all about you, Stephen. I'd be nothing without you. Well, why do they want me to have my own TV show, then?"

Me and my big mouth!

"What TV show?"

Instead of shutting up I carried on digging a hole for myself. "They want me and Malibu to be the British Kardashians," I said, as if I actually thought it was a good idea.

Stephen let out a loud groan.

"What's wrong with that?"

"Seriously?" he said. "Sex tapes and marrying people for seventy-two days and yer asking me what's wrong with it?"

"The Kardashians earned sixty million dollars this year," I said defensively. I should have known that wouldn't impress him.

"You're right, Remy, I'm wrong. *They* should be my heroes. I need to stop admiring the skills of Lionel Messi and start making sex tapes. Aye, why don't we make one tonight? Post it on Facebook. Is that what you want?"

A text from Malibu came through: *So what happened?!!* Ugh!

We went to bed and slept facing opposite walls.

Just about said hello to each other when we woke up. Then when I was doing my face Stephen said, "Yer don't need make-up."

So I gave my usual reply. "Well, I had a face full of it when you met me."

It's our little joke and he smiled just like normal. "There's a pre-season game on Saturday, if yer want to come."

"Sure."

So that's it – we've officially made up. Problem is,

I haven't figured out what I want. It was so easy before, being a big, bossy salon owner, dreaming about building a beauty empire. But now it feels like I've been given this opportunity to be famous, and everyone would think I was stupid if I wasted it. And then there's Scotland…!

Anyhoo, I've come home and booked an emergency session with Dr Clein to help me work it out.

10.45 a.m.

Just had a good talk with Mum. She said that she only sent Dad divorce papers because she needs closure and Dad deserves the same.

"Why didn't you tell me?"

"Alan thought you'd be upset."

"And how do *you* feel?"

"Sad."

"Mum, are you *sure* you want to get divorced?"

"Yes, love… It's for the best. It's closure."

2.30 p.m.

Arranged to meet Kellie for a quick catch-up at Nando's (our spiritual home). Spoke to Mal before I left.

"You were right, he does want me to live with him!" I gushed.

"Knew it! I'm so happy for you!"

There was no point adding "in Scotland". She would've

clicked that would be the death of *Being the Bennets* and I would never have got out of the house.

Camilla phoned when I was making my way over to Nando's. She asked me to do a phone interview today with *The Mutts* (apparently a v. popular mag with dog lovers).

"It's not *Life Stories* though, is it? I thought that's what we were going for?"

"Still working on it, dahling. But *The Mutts* is *really* quite prestigious… Prestigious means—"

"I know what prestigious means," I snapped. "How many readers has it got?"

"Erm … not sure but *a few*. And we have a couple of other big things waiting to be confirmed."

"TV things?" I asked.

"I don't want to say, dahling, in case I jinx them. But I do think that you'll be very, very happy once you find out."

I told her I was meeting a friend and I'd do *The Mutts* interview after that. Then it was Kellie time. Since she's started uni, an hour with Kellie is like reading *Fifty Shades of Grey*. I actually felt like I needed a good wash afterwards to cleanse my soul.

She asked how it was going with Stephen and I told her about possibly moving to Scotland.

"Scotland?! It's not really you, is it?"

"I dunno. Loved it when he took me to the Highlands. It was so beautiful, Kel."

"But what's there to do? Oh, I know…" Kellie put on

a girly American voice. "You gonna be a good little wife, cooking dinner, making the beds, and teaching Effie and Dougie how to bake."

"Don't you start," I said, but I couldn't help laughing.

I suppose she has got a point though – what *would* I do there?

Kel reminded me that as soon as she realized Stephen's teammate, David Joseph (who she saw for a while), was after a Stepford wife she "stepped off".

"Yeah, right," I said. "And it had nothing to do with him finding out that you were hooking up with Mark Carter behind his back."

She shrugged. "Uni does that to you, Rem."

"What, turns you into a slut?" I said cheekily.

She ignored the jibe. "No. Makes it hard to sustain a proper relationship."

"You couldn't sustain one *before* you went – remember?"

"What about Jack?"

"Oh yeah, Jack – I liked him."

"So did I. It's just that I liked a few others as well." She laughed.

Anyhoo, I told her that I probably wouldn't even be considering going to Scotland if I still had James in my life and she hadn't deserted me for uni.

"So call James, then."

"Nah. It's been too long. Best to leave it."

Just finished having the most ridiculous conversation with a journalist from *The Mutts* magazine.

"What's the name of your dog?" he asked.

"Er... I don't have one."

"Camilla said you did – that's why we've agreed to do this interview."

"Well, I don't know why because I don't."

"Perhaps you had one that recently died?"

"No, I've never had a dog. To be honest, I'm more of a cat person."

"Oh, *cats*," he said in disgust. "Well, shall we *pretend* you have a dog?"

"Erm... I don't think so. No."

He said he'd have to get on to Camilla, and rang off in a strop.

WTF?

7.55 P.M.

My Life: one step forward; two blooming back.

Had a great session with Dr Clein. He is one smart dude. I told him how gutted I'd been about Dad getting divorce papers. He took notes. Then he listened when I described the panic attacks I'd had before and during the meeting with Robert Fitzgerald. He took notes. Then he listened and nodded as I replayed last night's argument with Stephen, blow by blow. He took more notes, and didn't speak until I said, "I just hate the way he shot down my *Being the Bennets* idea."

"Remy, three days ago *Being the Bennets* was Malibu's idea and you didn't seem particularly keen on it. Now you're claiming it's yours. In fact, at the time you didn't seem sure that you liked being famous. What's changed?"

I searched for an answer and all I could come up with was "Everyone's going to think I'm an idiot if I waste this opportunity."

"They might, but you have to live your life for *you*, Remy. Do the things that matter to *you*. Even if everyone in the whole world rates fame – if *you* don't, you'll never be happy with it."

He was right. When I look back, Stephen has been the only good thing about this year; and maybe the salon (but I've hardly been there). Everything else has made me unhappy. I've lost count of how many times I've cried at the abuse I've received on Twitter; then of course I lost it on live TV; and then I had those panic attacks yesterday. This new career that Camilla and Harry are busting a gut to save – I don't like it. I don't like being gawped at and judged, or not being able to go out without make-up on because I'm so paranoid about being papped. And so what if I'm living Malibu's dream? It isn't *my* dream. I want to live for ME again. As I said all this aloud it made perfect sense. I told Dr Clein that the best thing for me to do was to forget about fame, and I instantly felt ten stone lighter. (No need for lipo any more, ha ha ha!)

"I'm contracted to do one more photo shoot for Terri Catalogue and then that's IT – back to being a very happy nobody," I said.

"What will you do instead?"

I smiled. "Move to Scotland."

And quite possibly open a new salon. ☺

Left Dr Clein and jumped into a taxi, full of confidence. Knew exactly what I was going to do.

Plan of Action

* Tell Stephen to go for his transfer.
* Tell Mal "Being the Bennets" is not for me.
* Keep her sweet by still buying a flat, and letting her live in it. (Also v. good investment.) All she'll have to do is pay bills.
* To help pay bills will ask her to replace me at Tah-dah! She was v. popular at Kara's and is bound to get her old customers back.
* Ask Stephen to invest in new salon in Scotland as "business partner" ← Eek! This is properly freaking me out. Business goes wrong = kills relationship. Relationship goes wrong = kills business. Adds a lot of pressure to moving to Scotland. ☹ ☹

Was trying to work out whether I should even ask Stephen to co-own a salon when Lara called.

"Are we allowed to use the kitty money to send flowers?" she asked.

"Not usually. Why?"

"Debbie Wyatt's in hospital."

"What happened?" I asked, surprised.

"Checked herself in to get help for depression."

But just the other day she was showing off her toyboy. "What? She seemed to be doing so well."

"I think she thought, deep down, that she and her hubby would get back together, but he's told her he wants a divorce."

My mind jumped to Malibu. *Mum thinks she's postnatal, doesn't she? Does that mean that crushing* Being the Bennets *will drag her even further down Depression Road?*

"Sure... Send Debbie some flowers."

I rang off, and before I knew it I was clutching a familiar pain in my chest and fighting for air.

"Are you all right love?" The taxi driver pulled over. He was brilliant. He wanted to call for an ambulance but I told him not to bother. "Are you sure?" he asked, concerned. So I nodded and gasped that I knew what it was.

"It'll stop in a minute. I just need to take big breaths."

It took a while to calm down and he looked relieved when it did. "Thought you were having a heart attack."

"I'm sorry. It happens sometimes."

"You'll need to get it looked at. Promise you will," he

told me when he pulled up outside my front door.

Dr Clein had said the same thing before I'd left his treatment room, adding that my GP might be able to give me some medication to keep me in check. The thought of medication scared me – I've seen *One Flew Over the Cuckoo's Nest*.

"Won't need any," I'd assured him. "Now I've decided to go to Scotland, I won't get stressed any more."

Now look at me – I'm a big, panic-attack-ridden loser! ☹

Friday 9 August – 9 a.m.

I am Remy Louise Bennet. I am not perfect. Blah, blah, blah.

Last night I suddenly wondered *What if I'm not a drama queen after all but at death's door?!* So when Stephen called to check if I was OK, I said I'd go round to his house. Lying in his arms would be the perfect place to pop my clogs.

This morning I lay in bed while he got ready for training. So far, there had been no mention of moving to Scotland. I think he wanted to concentrate on smoothing things over rather than starting another argument, and he knows it's a big ask. If I am missing a sensitivity chip, Stephen must have twenty. He also happens to have a v. v. fit body. ☺

I whistled as he got into his trackie bottoms.

"Aw, I'm just a piece of meat ter yer, aren't I."

"Yep, and don't you forget it!"

Grinning, he said, "That pre-season match is tomorrow – yer still coming?"

"Of course I am."

"Right. Better get yer a ticket then."

"Thanks. And baby, you can put in for that transfer if you want."

His face was a screenshot of pure joy. Then he turned serious. "Are yer sure, gorgeous? I don't want ter force yer."

"I'm positive. I *want* to go. Let's live in Scotland!"

He kissed me.

"I love you," I told him, just in case it was for the last time. *slowly plays violin*

7.45 a.m.

Finished my make-up, booked an appointment with my GP, then decided to phone James. Yikes! I was so–oo nervous.

"I miss you," I said before he could hang up. "Sorry for accusing Rupert of spiking my drink. He—"

"Is a tosser," James cut in. "Don't worry, Remy, I've seen the light."

"So you're not going out with him any more?"

"Haven't done for ages. He's so bloody up himself it's untrue."

"Yeah, I did notice." I laughed.

"And Rem, I want to apologize for being up myself too.

Believe me, I've missed you more." James said he was desperate to be accepted by the cool set in Shoreditch back then, but it was actually exhausting. "I'm always going to like Britney and Kylie. I know it's a stereotype, as Rupert kept telling me, but that's just me – and what's the point in pretending when I'm with *other* gay people?"

James isn't even working in Shoreditch any more. He's joined a new salon in the West End.

"Yay!" I said. "In that case, I'm coming to get my hair done. It's the only reason I've made up with you – far too many bad hair days."

"User."

We laughed.

"How are things with your parents?"

"Fine."

"Great. That worked out, then."

"Oh no, I haven't told them yet." Last year he came close to telling them he was gay more times than I can count. He never managed it though. "But I'm going to next week for definite. I've met someone. Actually, I'm in *lurve*."

I could tell he was beaming.

"Who with?"

"Don't know what's going to shock my dad the most – the fact that I'm gay or the fact that I'm seeing his boss's son."

"No. Way."

Apparently his dad's boss had a barbecue and as his

dad was up for a promotion, he wanted to make a big impression and forced James to go. Little did his dad know that James happened to spot that the boss's son, Dominic, was "beyond gorgeous" as soon as he'd opened the front door. Seems he's a real sporty/rugby type. An hour into the barbecue they were in the downstairs toilet kissing.

"*Classy*. Don't know who's worse, you or Kellie," I said.

We chuckled together for a bit. Felt like old times.

"So, come on, tell me – what's it like to be a celebrity?" he asked.

For a second I thought about pretending, to avoid the "But you're so lucky. You should appreciate it, blah, blah, blah." But what was the point?

"Shit," I replied.

"No way. It can't be!"

"Yes, it can. Especially when you're getting tons of insults on Twitter all the time. In fact it makes me feel so shitty I'm seriously considering giving it up."

"Well, get on with it, then. Because if there's anything I've learned this year, it's that life is too short."

"Tell me about it." I sighed.

Great speaking to my BMF @James1Hair today. Now we have to go out with @Kelz #goodtimes #backforgood

Camilla Douglas-Smith phoned when I was on the way home from Stephen's.

"Dahling, what happened with *The Mutts* interview?"

"Um… He called, asked about my dog, I said I didn't have a dog, and then he said he'd phone you."

"Oh God, I worked my ahse off to get you that interview."

"But if I don't have a dog, what am I supposed to do?"

"Well, you're *not* supposed to tell him that you're a cat person. Dog people *hate* cat people. It's taken me an age to smooth that over. Now, do you know anyone who *does* have a dog?"

I thought about it, then remembered that Grandma Robinson had just got one. A Yorkshire terrier. Bitten Dad twice already – it's almost as gangsta as she is.

"There you go," said Camilla. "Just pretend that your grandmother's Yorkie is yours. Can you do that for me, dahling?"

"I don't understand what's so important about *The Mutts*, Camilla. I thought we were going for *Life Stories*?"

"Yes, we are but every little bit helps. I'm not saying that *The Mutts* is little, of course, because it's huge – *huge* – among the dog-loving community, many of whom happen to work in television. You'll instantly win their respect. It's all about planting the right seeds in the right places."

Did the stupid *The Mutts* interview in the back of the

cab. Although I don't know why the journalist believed I was suddenly a huge dog fan. When I finished the call I thought, *One of the best bits about dumping celebrity life will be getting rid of the Camillas that infest the showbiz world.* Actually, I decided that Camilla's call was a blessing because it put me in the perfect mood to tell Malibu that I was bailing out of *Being the Bennets.* For the sake of my karma, I'd even worked out a nice way to tell her. But when I stepped into the house, Mal was so excited I thought she was going to wet herself.

"Have you spoken to Robert Fitzgerald yet?"

"No. Why?"

"Oh my God, it's ama–aazing news! He said ITV are interested."

"But… They can't be."

"They *are*! Robert's set up a meeting for next Wednesday."

12 P.M.

Spoke to Suzy, just to make sure I was doing the right thing moving to Scotland.

"Suzy, how hard was it to leave your family behind to come to London?"

"It was kinda exciting because I'd always wanted to see Europe. You know, I just love the royal family, especially William and Kate. I'd love to meet William and

Kate – they're just so awesome."

"Yeah, but don't you miss your family?"

"Sometimes, but there's Skype. I figured out some time ago that as long as I have Pootzy, I'm fine."

"Suzy and Pootzy" is their couple name. Ew!

"You goin' to the game tomorrow?" she asked.

"Yes."

"Great, I'll tell Oscar to make sure we're sitting together. What are you gonna wear?" Suzy never shows side-boob, bra straps or too much leg, and believes British girls dress inappropriately. *boo*

I, however, am willing to drop my Britishness on this occasion. "Dunno. Something … classy." We will be a vision of modesty but for completely different reasons: Suzy because – OK, Mal and Kel have a point – she rocks granny chic. Me because I'll never risk exposing a thong sandwich again!

4.30 p.m.

Dr Sharma did her bit with the stethoscope and then told me I had the resting heart rate of an athlete. Woo-hoo!

"The erratic beating you described may be down to stress," she said.

No shit.

"Are you stressed?"

"You could say that, yeah."

"I saw the YouTube clip," she admitted.

I blushed.

"My children keep me up to date with celebrity gossip," she took great pride in telling me. "Now work on staying calm. If not, I can prescribe you something."

"No, thanks," I said. I don't expect to be stressed for much longer. Not in the Highlands.

Went to the salon after the doc's and as soon as I arrived Lara asked for a talk.

"Remy, I feel like I'm much more than a beautician. So I'd like to have a share in the salon's profits."

"What?"

"Well, I am running the salon – you said so yourself."

"Did I?"

"Yes."

"Ri–iight. Give me a few days to think about it, then. OK?"

Me and my big mouth. Aa–aaargh!

Can't afford to lose her, especially if I'm going to Scotland. Now I'm off home, about to work out a deal that'll please Lara, me, Dad AND Uncle Pete. I may be some time... ☺

<u>5.45 P.M.</u>

OK, so I made the mistake of checking Mail Online. Oops! One hour later... (It's the celeb pictures, they always suck me in – plead with me to click on them!) Anyhoo, thank God I did, as it meant I was online when an email came from the Highland Manor. It was just about special offers on salon treatments, but that reminded me of something. Called them straight away and, as I'd hoped, they're still looking for someone to manage the place. They asked me to send my CV and an application form. The pressure of me moving to Scotland, and Stephen joining a new club, will be bad enough – but if I get the job I can put off asking him to invest in a salon for at least a year. #buyingtime ☺

Downloaded and printed the application form, filled it in, and have just been to the post office to send it Special Delivery (not taking any chances). Scotland, here I come!

6.45 P.M.

The calculations have fried my brain – but I genuinely think I have a solution for the salon that will please everybody.

It's Gary's weekend – he's just been to collect Gary Junior. Me, Malibu, Mum and Alan gathered in the hall-way to say goodbye as if we weren't going to see the little munchkin for years.

"Be good," I told him. He gave me a cheeky grin.

"He's always good for *me*," Gary replied. "I set boundaries."

That got Malibu going. "Well, maybe if a *certain person* was around more, I would too."

"What difference does it make?" Gary snapped back.

"Why should I be the one shouting and screaming at

him, while you play the good guy, taking him out and buying him treats?"

When both Garys left, I asked Malibu what she was going to do with her night off. "Fuck all," she said, then she went into her room and slammed the door.

I listened out for crying so I could go in and put my arm around her if needed. If she *is* on the brink of depression, I'm going to do whatever is needed to prevent it. Maybe even surrender to *Being the Bennets* – whatever it takes.

"Who d'you think you are, talking to me like that in front of my family!" I heard her screech into the phone. "I don't care any more. You're out of order... It's not easy looking after him, you know, while you're lording it up in your mansion. And if you don't start giving me more maintenance, I'm taking you to court!"

I was quite proud of her for ripping into him about the maintenance money, but when she ended the call she was sobbing.

"I hate my life!" she suddenly shouted at the top of her voice.

I went in to console her.

"It's OK, I'll be all right," she said, quickly wiping her eyes.

When she calmed down, I went to Mum and told her that Mal needs to make an appointment with Dr Sharma.

"What for?"

"To check whether she's ... stressed."

"We don't need to check whether she's stressed – we *know* she's stressed."

"Well, maybe … Dr Sharma can prescribe something to help."

Phoned Stephen after that. The match tomorrow kicks off at 3 p.m. Haven't been to Netherfield Park for ages. After having the whole of last season off, I must be looking forward to hanging out with Suzy because I'm surprisingly excited about going. Stephen didn't believe me when I told him that though.

"Yer don't have to go that far, Remy."

"Have you asked for the transfer?" I checked.

"Naw, I wanna shine tomorrow to keep Celtic interested. And to do that, I have to be selected. But there's naw way I'll be picked if I ask for a transfer."

Bloody hell, football sounds like chess.

10 P.M.

Went to check on Malibu. She said that her one stupid mistake with Lance has made Gary hate her.

"Sometimes he looks at me and I can see the disgust on his face."

"Maybe it's not disgust. Maybe it's hurt because he still loves you."

"He's just so angry all the time! He says that even if he forgives me and moves on, how could he convince his friends and family that I'm not a leech or a gold-digger. A leech?! I'm nothing like that, Rem. I genuinely love him for who he is, and I still would even if he drove a bus."

"*You* with a bus driver – that wasn't part of the WAG Charter!" I laughed. Oops, clearly have a bit of work to do re sensitivity chip.

"That was just a bit of fun." Mal started to cry. "Lance is a builder and I would've easily ended up with him. But I met Gary and I chose Gary because I loved him more."

"Have you told him that?" I asked.

"Of course I have, then he goes and calls me a leech." She angrily wiped the tears away. "You wait, when this TV show comes off and makes us rich, I'm going to shove it in all their faces."

"Yeah, you do that," I told her.

Doh! Talk about making it hard for myself.

I then suggested that we chill out by watching a film. "How about *The Wolf of Wall Street*?" A chance for me to coo over Leo D.C. *and* cheer Mal up – perfect. ☺

Saturday 10 August – 9.15 a.m.

I am Remy Louise Bennet. I am not perfect … and I woke up hoping Malibu would understand that as much as I want to spare her from depression, I really don't want to do the TV show. I'm going to have to tell her. The question is, *when*?

Mal, Mum and Alan were sitting in silence when I went down for breakfast. Obviously something was going on.

"If I were you, I'd appreciate the fact you have a healthy little nipper," huffed Alan after a while.

"Like I said," replied Malibu, "keep your opinions to yourself."

"Malibu, that's enough now," Mum said sharply.

Silence again. I made myself some toast and sat down to eat it.

"No wonder you can't lose weight when you keep on eating that kind of rubbish!" snapped Malibu.

"What, toast and jam?"

"*Carbs* and *sugar* – everyone knows both were put on this earth by the devil."

"A bit like Gary Junior," I joked, attempting to lighten the mood. Mum gave me THE eyes. "Er... You know... Cos he's a cute little devil... Isn't he?"

Mal burst into tears. In the past twenty-four hours she has shed enough tears to fill the River Thames. Methinks depression is now a reality.

"It's my fault," she blubbed.

"He's not a devil, Mal, I was just joking."

"Junior's an angel."

"*Exactly* – fell straight from the sky."

"But I've ruined his life, and mine. You don't know how lucky you are, Remy. You're getting a second chance – make sure you don't fuck it up."

Didn't know whether she meant a second chance with Stephen or my celebrity career, but wasn't about to ask. She dropped her head to the table. Mum got up and stroked her hair; I rubbed her back. Alan looked awkward and picked up the newspaper. "Get her to Dr Sharma," I mouthed over her head. Mum nodded. When the crying died down, I said, "You're a catch, Mal, and if Gary doesn't realize it, he can jog on." That drew a faint smile. "Now, why don't you let me spoil you with some treatments at the salon?"

Just called Lara. The beauticians are fully booked this morning, so I'm going to swing by and do the treatments myself. ☺

1.30 p.m.

On the way to Netherfield Park Stadium. EEK!

Took full advantage of making up with James by calling him for some hair advice. I need to look perfect because unless the WAGs have had surgery on their personalities (along with their boobs), they are definitely going to judge me. He told me to go for the Croydon facelift, which is when you pull your hair into a pony-tail as tightly as you can – so tight your cheekbones rise, Kate Moss style. It's not as simple as it looks; it took for ever and loads of hair gel to get it right. I then felt para-noid about my face being so exposed. So I slapped on some extra make-up – more blusher with a bit of shading underneath and highlighter on top, to contour my face. Massive improvement, but still way too much face on show. Problem is, it's too late to pull my hair out and start again, so I've had to add even more blusher, highlighter, shading. *sigh*

The good news is, I have a sister who didn't shed a

tear during her facial and mani-pedi. That's two hours: RESULT.

When I finished her facial, Mal said she had flash-backs about working in Kara's. Aha! Perfect time to tell her my plan about running Tah-dah!, methought. Till she added, "And I never wanna wax someone's privates again." DISASTER.

Anyway, I need to forget all that for now and con-centrate on the game. Will hopefully have a v. happy boyfriend after it, and he says we'll go out clubbing if he wins: RESULT.

Trouble is, Suzy and Pootzy will refuse to go if Angus is going too (due to previous experience at Whisky Mist). DISASTER.

"The guy's bad news," said Suzy when I called to say I was running a bit late.

I don't feel as strongly as she does, but he can be a pain. Just sitting beside him for the match today is an overdose of Angus in my opinion.

"Why don't I tell Stephen to make it a couples' night."

"Can you, sweetie?"

"Sure."

Doesn't mean Stephen's going to listen though.

<u>8 P.M.</u>

At the flat of a semi-happy boyfriend.

The team won: Yay!

Stephen scored: Double yay!

But twot-face Robbie scored twice: Sucks big time!

Decided to wear a black maxi dress, and hoped that Suzy would approve; she may not be perfect but she's good to have in your corner when you're up against the Netherfield WAGs. Suzy doesn't have a good word to say about any of them.

"Here comes our bodyguard," she whispered as Angus made his way to his seat next to us. (She doesn't have a good word to say about him either.) "And look at his freaking teeth – no wonder he can't get a job."

I think Angus's teeth offend her the most. Admittedly they don't say glamorous American, but they're nowhere near the level of the average guest on *The Jeremy Kyle Show*. #justsaying

"Great day for it, girls," he boomed as he sat down.

Yep. Today was the hottest day of the year so far. Yippee! I'd passed a shedload of ice-cream vans on the way to the stadium, already seen four FB posts about barbecues, and gawped at numerous happy, inappropriately dressed people with wobbly bits wobbling as they bounced down the street. Hey folks, if my bum causes earthquakes, at least today proves I am not alone. ☺

Unfortunately for Suzy, that meant the Netherfield Park WAGs proudly had their extremely un-wobbly, rock-hard silicone bits on show. I suppose they've worked hard (or, in some cases, paid) to get their perfect bodies, and today was an opportunity to show them off. BIG TIME. Anyhoo, they sparked endless tutting from "Granny".

"You look classy," I said, admiring her white trouser suit.

"Thanks. You look pretty awesome too."

Oh yeah – Suzy says "awesome" a lot.

People are still away on holiday so the stadium was only three-quarters full. Pre-season games aren't usually important but I felt nervous for Stephen – his chance to play for Celtic was at stake. And as for Angus, I'm sure he'd chewed off all his fingernails barely ten minutes into the match! When Stephen scored, all three of us jumped out of our seats and hugged each other.

"Way to go, Stevie!" shouted Suzy.

"Ye–eeeees. Stick it ter them, Stevie boy!" roared Angus.

"So, will *he* live with you guys when you move to Scotland?" Suzy leant in to whisper.

I was shocked she knew about Scotland. "Stephen told Oscar," she explained.

I was glad it hadn't been down to my big mouth, but it still ruined any chance of me enjoying the rest of the game. I hadn't considered Angus moving in with us. I tried to convince myself that he wouldn't – surely Stephen would've mentioned it?

"No," I whispered back. "At least … I don't think so."

"*You don't think so*," she hissed. "Man, if I were you, I'd get that straight, right away!"

The manager subbed Stephen fifteen minutes after his goal.

"Why did he do that?" I asked.

"Favouritism," griped Angus. "Hopefully he won't have ter put up with it fer too much longer."

Robbie then ended up scoring twice, as I said, and the match finished three–nil. I don't feel anything for Robbie any more – he doesn't even deserve my hate – but I still blush when people stare to see my reaction. Especially when it's Suzy. "Are you OK?" she asked each time Robbie scored.

"I'm awesome," I said after the second goal.

In the players' lounge, instead of snubbing me like they'd done the last time I was there, some of the WAGs gathered round to say hello. Charlotte, Becky, Danielle... They looked proper excited to see me.

"Have you heard from Paris?" I asked Charlotte. She shook her head. "No, me neither."

Charlotte said Paris is probably still gutted about being dumped by Terry Dawson for a pair of pole-dancing twins (one for him, the other one is going out with Robbie). That's just so predictable of those two. They're cardboard cut-out footballers.

I chatted with the WAGs, but every now and then I reminded myself that I'm the same person they hated so much before. The only difference is that I've now been seen on the sixty-inch HD plasma hanging on their living-room wall. And it isn't just them; loads of people who used to hate me are suddenly following me on Twitter and requesting to be my Facebook friend. Even after years of bullying, Tara (spit, spit) Reid still had the front to try and "friend" me. I pressed the IGNORE button so hard I nearly made a hole in my iPad. It's proper hard to tell who's genuine any more.

On the drive back to Stephen's, Harry phoned to say how well he'd played. Apparently the Celtic rep he brought with him was v. impressed, so Stephen was in great spirits by the time we got back to his flat.

"Excuse us a minute, Angus," he said. Then he dragged me to his room and gave me a long snog.

"Are yer sure yer ready for the move?"

I'd thought about it all afternoon and I didn't think I could do it if Angus was going to live with us – that would be a deal-breaker for me.

"I'd like to, babe, but what are we going to do about Angus?"

He sighed. "I don't know yet."

I could tell he was torn, and I finally understood: looking out for Angus is Stephen's duty, just like looking out for Mal has become mine. We're a right pair.

"Let's not worry about that fer now. Let's all go out and get something ter eat and then I'll phone Mike and ask him ter get us into Whisky Mist."

My body froze. "Can we make it a couples' night out?"

"What about Angus?"

"Erm… He can stay here – watch a film or something," I suggested.

"He'd be bored."

"Well, Oscar and Suzy won't come, then."

Stephen was surprised. "Why not?"

"Remember last time – when Angus was up for starting World War Three?"

"Aw, that won't happen again."

"Well, can you at least have a word with him to make sure?"

"Awkay, gorgeous."

Then Stephen rang Mike Monroe. Mike's connected; he knows the owners of all the top clubs in London. Some of them are quite snooty about who they put on their guest lists, but Mike always makes sure we can get in.

"Is your mate going to be there – the *big* one?" he asked.

"Aye."

"He's got to behave himself this time, then."

"Sure. Naw problem."

Mike called back to say a VIP table had been arranged. I have to admit, being a celebrity has its perks.

"Babe, are you a hundred per cent sure you want to bring Angus?"

"Yes–ss!"

"Just checking."

Anyhoo, decided to invite Malibu too. (Can slyly work on her about the Tah-dah! job while we're out.)

"A bunch of loved-up couples are the last thing I want to be around," she said.

"Don't worry, Angus is coming too."

"Oh, go on, then."

Think I've earned myself an epic night out! #woohoo

Angus has been arrested!

Stephen keeps claiming it's Malibu's fault but that's just a cop-out – she's not the one who knocked a man senseless. (I think I even heard *splat* when the guy hit the floor.) OK, I can't deny that Malibu was a real handful last night, because she was. A proper nightmare. She got so bad that in the end I switched to drinking water just to make sure I was sober enough to look after her. Not that it helped. Nobody could've controlled her. It was as if MI5 had set her a mission: to get absolutely, completely wasted, and not even James Bond was going to beat her to it.

In my opinion, there are three kinds of drunk: happy, aggressive and downright miserable. Somehow, Malibu managed to become all three.

"Tu–uuuuune!" she cried when "Time of My Life" by Black Eyed Peas came on, even though she's always said it's their worst song ever.

Her arms were flying all over the place. People scattered as if she were holding a grenade. Meanwhile, I tried very hard to act like she was invisible.

"Your sister's having a great time, huh?" Suzy commented. The rest of us were still sat at our VIP table, trying to salvage the little amount of vodka Malibu had left in the bottle. "Is it the first time she's been out since having the baby?"

"Er … no. The second time. We went to a charity ball last week."

"Awesome."

At this point, Malibu was definitely having a good time. Taking selfies and uploading them to Facebook with uber-happy messages underneath to make Gary burn: "Par–rrty time!" "Having the best time EVER!" "YOLO!"

But then she became aggressive. An aggressive drunk has issues – being messed around by the father of her child, in Malibu's case – and if the person they have issues with isn't present, they find a reason to take it out on someone else. That would be you, blonde girl who accidentally spilt your drink on Malibu's dress. *I* understand that it wasn't your fault and that it only happened because of Malibu's flailing arms, knocking the glass out of your hand. But, unfortunately for you, you were dealing with Malibu Bennet.

"You stupid bitch!" Malibu screamed loud enough to drown out the music.

"Erm, is your sister all right?" checked Suzy.

"Yeah, yeah, she's … awesome."

She so wasn't. And all it took was a song … *their* song, more importantly – "We Found Love" by Rihanna – to move her to stage three: downright miserable. She staggered back to our table, two mascara canals streaming down her face.

"Do you reckon he's found someone else, Rem?"

"No, Mal."

"He has, hasn't he?"

"No."

"That bastard."

OK. Change of tactics. "Yeah, he's a bastard, Mal. Forget him. Move on."

"But he's *my* bastard though *sob* and I love him."

New tactic: "OK, well go for it, then. Let him know how you feel."

"But do you reckon he's found someone else?"

I could tell Stephen felt sorry for me. "Come on, let's drink up. It's time to go home."

The dance floor was packed by then and someone with four-inch spiked heels, made a huge mistake by stepping on Malibu's toe, as we were making our way out. She shoved the girl, who went flying into what turned out to be a feisty drunk man, and he then sprang at Malibu and started screaming in her face. Cue our bodyguard. Angus got all Kevin Costner on his ass and grabbed him by his shirt. Feisty Drunk Man spat in his face – and that's when Angus knocked him out. *splat*

Feisty Drunk Man had two semi-aggressive drunk friends who wanted to defend their mate. They stormed up to Angus, threatening to do him damage, but when Angus shouted, "Come on, then – let's go, yer little pricks," they froze. So Angus decided to fight them anyway.

Girls screamed.

Suzy screamed. "I told you the guy's a psycho!"

Malibu screamed. "And *you* can shut up, you uptight old granny!"

Suzy screamed back, "Did you just hear what your sister said to me?"

Suddenly, four burly bouncers rushed in, grabbed Angus and dragged him away. The police were already outside and the bouncers handed Angus over to them.

"Please, guys," Stephen pleaded, "just tell them it was mistaken identity and bring him back."

"It was self-defence!" Angus screamed as he was thrown into the back of the police van.

It was clearly too late to save him.

"Man, we're gonna be in huge trouble if this gets out," Oscar said to Stephen.

Suzy had other things on her mind. "Hey Malibu, what did you freaking call me back there?"

"A g-r-a-n-n-y," Malibu spelt out because she's g-a-n-g-s-t-a.

Anyhoo, I know enough about celebrity status by now to realize that by the time this incident is reported in the newspapers, it'll be "footballers Oscar Raymond and Stephen Campbell and meltdown queen 'Bumquake' in fight". And Angus will get away with just a brief mention. None of this seemed to have occurred to Malibu. She had gone full circle and returned to happy drunk, giggling in the back of the cab on the way home.

"What a drama. No wonder they want to do a TV show about us, Rem. This would've been perfect for ratings!"

Stephen glared at me.

"Ha, ha, ha, *TV show*? Mal, you're so funny," I said, and

won't be waiting for an Oscar nomination.

The cab stopped at Mum's. Malibu slurred, "See ya later, guys," opened the car door and then staggered towards the house.

"Look at the state of her."

"Leave her alone, she's having a hard time."

"Well, I hope yer knaw Angus might get locked up because of *her*."

Stephen said that I'd better go in too, as there was no point going to his place – he's going to spend the night trying to find out which police station Angus has been taken to. ☹

4.05 a.m.

Called Stephen every half-hour for updates. The only thing we knew for sure was that we were both banned from Whisky Mist (Mike Monroe was the first person to call). We had no clue where Angus was.

"Wow. He'll do anything to live rent-free," I tried to joke.

Stephen wasn't having any of it. So it was good to hear the relief in his voice just now.

"Found him," he announced.

Apparently Angus is in Charing Cross police station and he's going to be detained overnight.

"He's been in trouble for fighting before," said Stephen with a sigh.

"No shit."

"They might sentence him this time. *Thanks to your sister.*"

"She's not the one who KO'ed someone!"

"He was trying to protect her!"

"And what about the other time when he almost flattened that weedy bloke?!"

"Yes. But he didn't, *did he*?"

"All right, calm down. I think I have a plan."

I'd called Kellie. Like proper besties we're still allowed to phone after hours if it's an emergency. And as she's destined to be a hotshot lawyer, I needed some advice asap.

"He needs to stick to his self-defence claim. All potential witnesses would have had one too many. That means their statements can't be trusted. So, it'll be hard to prove. He should get off," I told Stephen.

"You been speaking to Kellie?"

"Er… Yeah."

"Did she also tell yer that up until then, *my* name's going ter be torn to shreds in the papers?"

"Mine too, y'know."

"Aw aye. Perfect for yer TV show. *Great* for the ratings," he snapped.

"She was drunk!" I protested.

"Aw really? So are yer doing this show or not?"

"No, I'm not bloody doing the show!" I lowered my voice. These walls are proper thin and I didn't want Mal to hear me. "Look, it's complicated. I haven't managed to tell Malibu that I'm not up for it yet, that's all."

"Well, when will yer?"

"Soon. I have to time it right... *She's depressed*," I whispered.

Stephen reckons the story is bound to come out, so we agreed that he should call Harry. He's great when he goes into what he calls "clean-up mode" to protect his clients. So, fingers crossed.

9.30 a.m.

I lay in bed with the phone in my hand and dozed on and off until Stephen called back to say he'd spoken to Harry. I have to admit, I wasn't expecting football to be at the top of the priority list.

"Harry's worked out how to smooth things over with Netherfield Park *and* Celtic."

Stephen sounded ecstatic. Apparently people target players all the time. Sometimes they're rival fans or just jealous of the hero worship. The point is there's a whole gang of people who enjoy making trouble for a footballer, and that's how Harry wants us to play it.

"He says everyone's got to be singing the same tune – *and that includes yer sister.* Then he's going to phone a few friends in the media and plant a story about Angus protecting us from a Hawley United fan."

Hawley United are Netherfield Park Rangers' bitter rivals.

"But that's bullshit," I said.

"Do you want us to be crucified?"

Hmm. Good point.

"Just make sure yer sister goes along with it."

"OK–aay," I huffed, starting to feel sorry for Malibu.

Brekkie time: starving.

10 a.m.

Mum was sitting in the kitchen. Alan was by the toaster.

"Where's Mal?" I asked.

"Still in bed. How much did she drink last night? Popped my head round the door and she was dead to the world."

Something made me panic. What if she'd done something stupid? I ran upstairs and knocked on Mal's door… No answer. Knocked a bit harder… Nothing. Then banged my fists against it and finally burst into her room. She was lying in bed. Lifeless.

"Oh God! Mal! Mal!"

Suddenly her eyes flashed open. "Get the hell out of my room!"

Humph! To think I actually felt sorry for her a few minutes ago. Hope she goes to Dr Sharma, pronto, because she needs her head bloody checked! I'm sick of her. Said as much to Mum and Alan when I went back into the kitchen and told them about last night.

"You know she always gets touchy when Junior stays over at Gary's," said Mum.

"Alison, stop defending the indefensible," said Alan.

OK, Alan has his faults – having an affair with Mum (HIS BEST FRIEND'S WIFE) springs to mind – but he was right. "At last – someone in this house sees sense," I replied.

"Thank you, Remy," he said, surprised.

Mum glared at him.

"Well, I hope you know that it's *my* name that's going to be dragged through the mud – not *hers*," I said to Mum. Then I stormed off to my room in a strop.

10.30 a.m.

Mal came in to apologize. She looked a right state. Still pretty, of course, but pale – deathly pale – and the residue of last night's hairspray, combined with what must have been a lot of tossing and turning in bed, meant that sections of her hair were standing on end.

"I made a bit of a tit of myself last night, didn't I?"

"Um… You weren't at your best."

She looked embarrassed. "What happened to Angus?"

"They kept him in overnight. Hopefully, he won't go to prison."

"Oh shit."

"Look, if anyone asks, last night's fight was because a Hawley United fan tried to attack Stephen, OK?"

"OK. And… Tell him I'm sorry."

There wasn't anything she could do about it now so

I tried to make her smile. "What time's Gary Junior coming back?"

"How am I supposed to know? I'm not psychic!"

"Mal, you're so blooming moody all the time, it's doing my head in," I told her.

She said I would be in the same state if I hadn't been touched or kissed for months. "I'm not just a mother, you know. I'm a woman too!"

Yes. A very frickin' mardy one. ☹

Malibu sighed and sat down on the edge of my bed. "It's just that Gary doesn't seem to see that any more. Maybe it's nothing to do with Lance. Maybe it's because I've had a baby. Some girls at my NCT group have had their husbands go right off them after seeing them give birth. They say it's hard for them to get past seeing their wife's bits squeeze the equivalent of a melon through a pinhole. Not that Gary was there when I had Gary Junior..."

No, but I was. And thankfully, I stayed north. That was traumatic enough!

Stephen phoned about ten minutes later – Angus has been released and he's on bail while the police investigate the incident. He'll have to return to the station in a month to see whether he's charged. I offered to come over, but Stephen said that it's best to stay home until Angus calms down.

Gr–rrreat.

Felt like I was being punished, even though I wasn't the psycho who went ballistic! "So, have you decided what you're going to do about him?" I asked, feeling proper annoyed – meaning *when we move to Scotland*...

But Stephen replied, "Yep. I'm going ter get him somethin' to eat – he's always like this when he's hungry. I'll call yer when he's OK."

Meanwhile, what am I going to do? Can't exactly hang out with Miss Moody Knickers.

Aha! Will phone James and Kel, and see if they're up for doing something. #everycloud

10.55 a.m.

Woo-hoo! We're all going to meet for Sunday lunch. And James is bringing his new man. ☺

@Kelz @James1Hair See you soon, biatches! #reunion #bringiton

6 p.m.

Learnt loads today. First thing was that I am most definitely an adult. So is James. Kellie is only technically one.

We had a proper good talk about how we couldn't wait to be adults when we were younger. Thought we'd be able to do whatever we wanted: no parents ordering you about any more, etc. – woo-hoo! Thing is, when you're an actual adult you realize that you CAN'T do whatever you want because of an ickle thing called RESPONSIBILITY.

I have responsibilities towards my staff and clients at

the salon – plus Dad and Uncle Pete for giving me the loan. James has a responsibility to pay his rent to his brand-spanking-new landlord. Kellie, meanwhile, is pissing about at uni.

"Stop demeaning my life," she complained.

"We're not demeaning it, Kel, we're simply saying you don't have any responsibilities."

"Yes, I do. I have to pay for my student residence."

"And you'll have to pay off an enormous loan at the end," piped up James's boyfriend.

"That's right. Thank you, Dominic," Kellie said.

I really like Dominic. He's a handsome blond with a square jaw, superhero body and, most importantly, he's totally gaga for James. I've never seen James so happy. He's found himself a flat near the hair salon where he works. The next step is coming out to his parents, and then Dominic is going to move in.

"When Dad finds out, I'm sure he'll chuck me out. But now I have my own flat, that won't be a problem."

"Your dad wouldn't chuck you out," said Dominic. "It's *my* dad that we have to worry about. He's kept my sexuality a secret from everybody except close family, and he's never seen me in a relationship."

"What d'you think will happen?" Kellie asked.

"Oh, he'll probably stop talking to me for a bit. He did it for two months when I gave up rugby. Five, when I told him I was gay. Who knows, it might be a whole year this time – but you're worth it." He grinned.

James grinned back and gave him a quick peck on the lips. "The thing is, being an adult entails so many compromises. Picking your partner is one of the few choices that's *all* yours."

"Unless you're forced into an arranged marriage, of course," said Kellie. This is why she's going to be a lawyer: she's got a reply for everything.

"You know what I mean," James said, rolling his eyes. "And I know I can look Dominic in the eyes and say 'I'd choose you again and again, no matter what'."

I sighed. It's one of the most romantic things I've ever heard.

Dad texted when I was on the way home. Said he was in the King's Head for lunch with Elizabeth and wondered whether Mal and I wanted to stop by. I was surprised because he's never taken Elizabeth out so close to home before. I texted back: *Sure*. Then called Mal. She didn't want to come out.

"You can't stay moping around your bedroom all day," I said. "Go on, Mal – there'll probably be some fit blokes for us to gawp at."

"You've already got a bloke."

"I know. Just looking… For you. Ple–eeease."

"OK. Let me finish watching this thing on YouTube, then I'll come over."

When I got to the King's Head, I could tell that Elizabeth was bursting to tell me something. "Go on then, Reg, tell her."

Dad picked up her hand and said, "Elizabeth and I have decided to live together." He was beaming.

"Wow… That's great news," I replied.

"You can't keep a good woman waiting," he said, giving me a knowing wink.

I decided that now might be a good time to share my own news. "I've got something to tell you too… Celtic are keen on Stephen, and if he signs for them, he wants me to move up there with him."

"Oh Remy!" Dad was clearly surprised. "But are you *sure* you want to go? Don't get me wrong – Stephen's a great lad – but it's a lot to give up if you're not married. And you're going to be ever so far away if things go wrong."

"Dad, it's Scotland, not Timbuktu."

"And what are you going to do up there? What about the salon?"

"Please, Dad, I'll sort everything. I know my responsibilities."

Mal arrived thirty minutes later, saying she had a head-ache (surprise, surprise).

"Big night, then?" Dad asked.

"Yeah," she groaned.

"Good?"

"It was interesting…" I answered quickly.

"Mal, you should've stayed at home, love, if you feel that bad," Dad coaxed, then he told her the news about moving in with Elizabeth.

"I'm happy for you both," said Mal. "Maybe Elizabeth

could give us some tips on how to get *our* men to take the plunge."

Dad frowned at me, obviously confused. Oh-oh – time to tell Mal about moving to Scotland before I was busted. "Actually, there's er … something I—"

"Oh–hh my–yy bloody God." Mal was staring across the pub.

I turned and saw Lance "Heartbreaker" Wilson standing at the bar chatting to a couple of his mates, beer glass in hand. He gave us one of his slimy smiles, then had the audacity to come up to our table and ask Malibu outside for a chat.

"All right then," she agreed without hesitation.

WTF?!

I knew it was a bad idea but didn't expect her to come back crying.

"I need to go home," she said.

"I'll come with you." I quickly stuffed my Yorkshire pudding in my mouth (was saving it till last) and left behind the rest of what had turned out to be the best roast dinner ever. Proving that being an adult is also about SACRIFICE.

Mal was silent all the way home and went straight to her room as soon as we got in. Humph! When I went into the kitchen, Mum was sitting at the table in tears. What is it with the Bennet women at the moment?!

"What's the matter, Mum?"

She pointed to the official papers lying in front of her, wiped her eyes, picked up a pen and then slowly signed them. She looked up. "Divorce... It's so final, isn't it?"

That's adulthood: even when you choose your lifelong partner, you still might end up regretting it.

Genuinely hope Mum's made the right decision. Especially now Dad's moving in with Elizabeth.

7.30 P.M.

Gary Junior's back and Mal's in a much better mood! ☺

After she put him to bed she came into my room and said she couldn't wait until Wednesday (day of ITV meeting) because that was going to be the day she moved on with her life.

I could feel my heart rate speeding up. "Don't rely on that though, Mal. They might not want to do it. Maybe we should think up a plan B?"

She suddenly became the strong big sister that she used to be. "Don't worry," she said, hugging me tight, "they'll do it – we just have to believe." And then it was my turn to cry.

How can I get out of it now? ☹

8.30 P.M.

Need to leave. Feel so trapped in this house – it's an emotional minefield. Going to ring Stephen and see if I can go there.

Stephen said, "Don't think it'll be wise ter come round at the minute."

"Oh. I take it Angus is still angry then."

"'Fraid so."

"But I *need* to come over. He'll just have to get over it."

"I don't think yer should. We've still got a lot ter sort out."

"Haven't we agreed that we're going to blame a Hawley United fan?"

"Not about last night. It's about us moving to Scotland."

"Us…"

"Yes. I've let him know that he's going ter have ter find his own place. I want you and me ter make a proper start on our own."

I love him so—ooo much. ☺

Monday 12 August – 8.15 a.m.

I am Remy Louise Bennet. Blah, blah, blah.

Stayed in last night, after all, and must have fallen asleep by ten. Woke up with a great big smile on my face: I have the best man in the world.

Then I heard Malibu chasing Gary Junior down the passageway. "Come on, honey, Mummy needs to put on your nappy. Ple–eeeeease."

She sounds so happy. I am totally screwed. ☹

@MimiFitness mercy pleeeeeeease!

Got training with Mimi in fifteen mins. Ugh!

Fitted in loads today. First stop was the salon, and Dad called on the way. Harry planted the troublesome Hawley United fan story in at least three papers. Did a bloody good job too – made Angus look like a hero, and Dad was v. concerned. "Why didn't you mention it yesterday?" he asked.

"Um… Well…"

"Anyway, thank God you didn't get hurt. And I'm sorry if I didn't sound overly enthusiastic about Scotland. It's not definite yet though, is it?"

"No, but I think we need to have a meeting anyway. Will you and Uncle Pete be around tomorrow?"

They will be, so we're meeting at the King's Head.

Then had to deal with Lara. She wanted a private word as soon as I arrived. I knew what to expect.

"Have you thought any more about the salon manager job?"

"Well, I, er… Have had a lot on my plate."

"OK, but you should know that I've been offered a partnership at another salon. Obviously, I'd prefer to be here."

Shit. "Right. Well, thanks for letting me know. I should've made a decision very soon."

Got big news on the way to Dr Clein's – Celtic have made Stephen a firm offer.

"I've just handed in my transfer request. If all goes well, things'll be wrapped up in a week," he told me.

"A week?! I thought you said the end of August?"

"Well, I had until then to put in the transfer request, but if it's accepted I can sign for Celtic straight away."

"I'm so happy for you, baby!" I meant it, but so soon? Moving to Scotland had just become very real. OMG.

"We'll have to go house-hunting."

The joy of that thought wiped away my fears, but only for a moment.

"What about Angus?" I asked. "How's he going to find a place that fast?"

"Don't worry, he's already seen one he likes. He's meeting the estate agent in Glasgow on Wednesday."

"Oh. He's moving back to Glasgow then." I thought having Stephen to myself was too good to be true.

"Aye. Yer get more fer yer money up there."

"Didn't know Angus had any money! Has he won the lottery?" I joked. But Stephen didn't laugh. I suddenly twigged. "You're buying it for him, aren't you?"

"It's an investment," he explained. "It'll be in my name – he'll just live there."

"And pay you rent?"

"Eventually … when he finds himself a job."

Which, roughly translated, means never.

The thing is, I couldn't criticize because Stephen's only doing for Angus what I plan to do for Malibu. It's our duty, I suppose; and it's cheap at the price: A hundred grand

– that's nothing compared with the guilt he'd feel if he left Angus high and dry.

"How did Malibu take yer not doing the TV show, by the way?" he asked.

"Well... She, er... Um..."

"Yer haven't told her, have yer?"

sigh

Got to Dr Clein's and he said it was the happiest he's seen me.

"Yeah, I am happy, I suppose. There are just a couple of things I still need to sort out."

"And they are?"

"Telling Malibu I'm moving to Scotland. And that I'm not doing the TV show."

Dr Clein raised his eyebrows. "Good luck!"

I blooming well need it!

Then went to Terri Catalogue HQ to discuss my last photo shoot – the Remy L.B. bikini range. I said yes to everything they ran by me, thinking, *Who cares? This shizz is about to be over.* Harry, however, clueless about my celebrity retirement plans, kept banging on about Terri Catalogue offering me a new contract.

"If ya don't snatch her up again, she'll get a flood of new offers y'know. I've already had Littlewoods on the phone."

He was lying of course. OK, he had had Littlewoods on the phone *but*, he admitted once we'd left the building, they'd called about another of his clients.

"Still, that'll put the fear of God into 'em," he added.

Terri Catalogue haven't offered me a new contract yet because, so far, the sales of my clothes range have been crap. Or, as they put it, "Sales haven't been as expected." But now I understand what people in the celebrity world really mean when they say things. I'm like a bullshit code breaker. Anyhoo, they're hoping the bikini range will turn things round. With *my* backside modelling it? Oh Lawd!

6 P.M.

Mimi made me jump, skip, run and row.

"I'm not Jessica frickin' Ennis!" I protested.

"Do you want to look good in a bikini?"

"YES!" (She made me shout like an army cadet.)

"Do you want to do it in three weeks?"

"YES!"

"Then that takes dedication. Are you dedicated enough?"

"YES!"

"I *said*, are you dedicated?"

"YES!"

Mimi says I'll need to cut out all carbs: no bread, potatoes, rice and pasta. And I'm not supposed to even look at crisps or chocolate for three weeks. WTF?! Might as well be in prison!

To cheer myself up, when I got home I searched online for houses for sale in the Highlands. Houses surrounded by mountains and as far away as possible from paparazzi lenses

– bliss. That's when I received an email from the Highland Manor spa. They want me to come for an interview this Wednesday at 4 p.m. Shi–iiiiit. That's the day of the ITV meeting. But checked for flights to Glasgow anyway, as by then ITV should have rejected the show in an ever-so-nice "Sorry it's not quite for us" kind of way, and chucked us out by eleven. I could then jump into a taxi, catch the 2 p.m. flight to Glasgow, and be at Highland Manor for 4 p.m. So I emailed back to say yes and have just booked the flights. Yippee!

Right. Better tell Mum I'm moving to Scotland.

8 P.M.

Mum was completely surprised when I told her.

"How are you going to do this TV show if you're up there and Malibu's down here?"

"Mum, there isn't going to be a TV show."

"Really? Malibu said ITV are keen."

"It doesn't matter what ITV want because *I'm* not going to do it." I remembered what she'd said to me when she broke up with Dad. Now I finally understood. "I've tried to go along with what other people want, Mum, but I hate fame. I don't want any part of it. So now I'm going to do something for *me*."

I swear I saw tears come to her eyes. "I knew something was wrong. I thought I'd lost the old Remy for good – you'd changed that much." She threw her arms around me and

143

squeezed. "I'm so proud of you. Now we have to prepare because this is going to break your sister's heart." ☹

Tuesday 13 August – 9 a.m.

Spent the night at Stephen's. Just wanted to feel sure that I was doing the right thing. When he opened the door with his trademark smile, I knew I was. He's proper gorgeous when he smiles. Angus had cooked dinner – poached salmon with new potatoes, and salad on the side.

"This is a big move fer yer, Stevie boy. Yer got ter turn up ter Celtic looking fit."

Angus was much nicer to me than I expected. He actually apologized for the fight.

"How's yer sister doing?" he asked.

"Fine."

"Still single?"

He has no shame.

When we got ready for bed, I told Stephen about the job interview at Highland Manor tomorrow.

"I'm going to fly up there in the afternoon."

He looked surprised. "That's great, but yer don't have ter work, yer know. I'm making enough money ter—"

"Keep me?" I cut in.

By footballers' standards, we've had a strange relationship when it comes to money. Stephen has bought me loads of great birthday and Christmas presents – my black Louboutin pumps are my fave – but it's nothing compared with what the Netherfield WAGs are regularly showered with. I suspect it's because Rosie took Stephen for a ride, but I've enjoyed proving that I'm nothing like her. Besides, I've seen far too many WAGs trapped by the lifestyle.

"It's OK. I can look after myself," I told him.

Stephen didn't say anything.

When we woke up this morning, Stephen was dreading going to the club. Players who make a transfer request are treated like traitors. They're not allowed to train with the main players any more, and train with the kids instead.

"It's humiliating."

"Don't go in then."

"I have ter. I'm still contracted to Netherfield. And the deal might go wrong. I'm not a Celtic player until the contract's signed and I've passed my medical."

What?! The big emosh conversations with Mum and Dad might've been for nothing!

"So, are we going or not then?"

"Seventy per cent, yes."

"Seventy per cent?"

"Yes. But yer can't bank on it."

"Well, it would be nice to know – it's only one of the most important decisions of my life!"

He told me about a player who drove hundreds of miles to join another club on the last day of the transfer window and did an impromptu interview outside his "new" club, only for the offer to be withdrawn. He had to drive back to his old club in shame.

"That's so embarrassing."

He shrugged. "That's football."

1.55 P.M.

Proper chaotic morning. Went to the salon for treatments (need to look good for my interview tomorrow) but was constantly interrupted by phone calls to my mobile. Journalists were fishing for info because the papers were speculating about Stephen's transfer request.

"Sorry, no comment," I said to everything they asked – not that they were willing to accept that as an answer.

"But are you looking forward to living near the coast?" said one.

"No comment."

"Maybe it's Sunderland then – is that right?" said another.

"No comment."

"Won't you miss London?"

"No–oo comment."

"Have you met any of the Celtic WAGs yet?"

"No … comment." Nearly got caught out with that one, so decided to switch off my phone.

The journalists then bombarded the salon with calls instead.

"Could you please get off the line? It's for customers.

Thank you," Lara snapped at them like a pro. Which only confirmed what I'd already been thinking: Lara would be more than capable of running Tah-dah! for good. So I let her know that I'd like to make it official, for a share of the profits.

"I just need to clear it with my investors," I explained. "I'm meeting them today."

"Great. Can you let them know that I have a very good offer from another salon?"

She's always been a tough cookie.

Phoned Dad to confirm the meeting with him and Uncle Pete. We're going to our "office", the King's Head, at eight-thirty tonight.

Just before I ended the call, Dad said, "Stephen's all over the back pages this morning. Are you sure you're doing the right thing?"

"Oh, for Pete's sake, Dad – I'm *positive*."

It's unusual for me to snap at Dad, but I just want a little bit of support.

Meanwhile, just when I thought I'd done a great job of fobbing off the reporters, Mum called and said, "I think it's time to tell Malibu about Scotland. It'll be terrible if she's the last one to find out."

"I'm still only seventy per cent sure. It's not actually confirmed," I told her.

"That's not what the reporter said."

"What reporter?!"

"The guy from the *Evening Standard*… I forget his name now. Very nice – so well spoken."

"Mum, what did he *say*?"

"That I must be devastated about you leaving home. So I said that I was but I understood because Celtic are a great team."

"No–ooooo!"

"What? They are, aren't they?"

"It's supposed to be A SECRET!" I screamed.

"How was I supposed to know?"

8 P.M.

Uh-oh. Mum's slip-up meant that Stephen's move to Celtic was now all over the back pages of the *Evening Standard*'s late edition. They also decided to print my tweet about the Highlands from the other week. Only they made it seem like I'd tweeted it today:

His girlfriend, controversial WAG Remy Bennet, tweeted about Stephen's move: The Scottish Highlands are beautiful!

Aa–aaaargh! How do these journos sleep at night?!

Harry and Stephen have both phoned and given me a right rollicking. WTF?! I can't be expected to control a blooming grown woman. Got home in a proper bad mood.

"Let's prepare for the ITV meeting," Malibu said as soon as I got in. Gary Junior was peeping through her legs.

"Erm… Can't. Got to meet Dad."

"What for?"

"For, um … boring salon talk. And…" I took a deep breath and decided to man up. "I think *we* need to have a quick talk too."

"Sure. Do you want to do it in my room?"

My heart began to race. *Please don't have another panic attack*, I thought as I followed Malibu into her bedroom. Gary Junior spotted his Lego tower and promptly ran off to destroy it: a symbol of what I'm doing to her dreams.

"Mal, I think you should know… Stephen's been offered a job in Scotland."

"I heard! Are you all right? I feel so bad for you."

"Huh?"

"Once Stephen goes back to Scotland, it's obvious what's going to happen next – long-distance relationships never work. But I want you to know I'm here for you, OK?"

"Uh-huh."

"*So*, shall we talk ITV when you get back then?"

"Yeah… Sure."

And hopefully by then, I will have grown a great big pair of men's bits.

11 p.m.

Aargh, this has been a lo–oong day. Rushed to the King's Head to meet Dad and Uncle Pete. They both ordered pasta carbonara (my fave), but thanks to Mimi, I had to go for grilled chicken. #boring

"Hmm. This Lara girl – can she be trusted?" asked

Uncle Pete, once I told them the plan. *"Remy?"*

I'd been hypnotized by the sight of his plateful of pasta, ham and lovely, creamy, creamy sauce… "Huh?"

"This Lara. *Can she be trusted?*"

"I think so. She's blooming worked miracles with the salon. Makes running it seem easy. How's the, erm … pasta tonight?"

"Great. Best it's ever been."

"But we didn't invest in Lara, Remy," Dad ploughed in. "We invested in you."

"I know. Look, Dad, I can fly back and forth but it might be difficult if…"

"If what?"

"If I get this spa job."

Dad couldn't believe it – "You've already applied for a job? What about our investment? Where's your sense of responsibility?"

"I'm not happy about this," said Uncle Pete, laying down his fork.

"You going to finish all that?" I asked him.

"Stick to the bloody subject!" snapped Dad.

Anyways, they've refused to OK Lara being a part of the business until I confirm how I intend to oversee things. And, if they do accept her, Pete said that any percentage she gets in the business has to come from my share.

I hate RESPONSIBILITIES!

Definitely wasn't in the mood for Malibu and her ridiculous plans when I got home.

"So, the good cop, bad cop tactic worked before," she said, "and you know what they say – if it ain't broke…"

My head was too full after trying to find ways to convince Dad and Uncle Pete, so I just said, "OK–aay."

She's gone to bed now and I can't wait for this TV crap to end tomorrow with a big fat ITV executive NO.

Just want to get on with MY life.

Dear God, please let the leisure manager of the Highland Manor say, "You're hired!"

Wednesday 14 August – 7.30 a.m.

Big, big day today!

Already had my protein-heavy breakfast: two hard-boiled eggs. Gross. Their smell made Gary Junior run away from the kitchen. I texted Mimi: *Are all carbs evil?*

Mimi: *Yes.*

Me: *Even Crunchy Nut Corn Flakes?*

Mimi: *ESPECIALLY Crunchy Nut Corn Flakes.*

Humph!

8 a.m.

Mal meditates! Burst into her room to borrow her straighteners and she was sitting on the floor CHANTING.

"Oops! Sorry, I should've knocked."

She didn't even flinch. "Nam-myoho-renge-kyo,

Nam-myoho-renge-kyo…"

Dr Sharma must have given her something STRONG.

When I was unplugging the straighteners, I noticed she'd pinned a v. small list to her bedroom wall, right above her dressing table. It said: Make a million. Marry Gary.

"I'll, um … see you soon?"

11.05 a.m.

On the way to the ITV Studios, Mal confessed that even she'd had enough of her mood swings.

"So you went to Dr Sharma?"

"*No.* I read a book. OK, I didn't read it but Evan Richards did and I went on his YouTube channel – that's why I was a bit late to meet you, Dad and Elizabeth the other day. He explains it so well, Rem. You write down the things you really, really want and then focus on them every day while you chant. It's worked for loads of famous people. It's a mix of Hinduism, Buddhism and *The Secret*."

The first two were probably the longest words I've ever heard her say. "Right. And d'you think it's working then?"

"Well, instead of moaning about what I want, I'm focusing on it instead. And I feel much happier." She smiled.

Wow. Been paying Dr Clein a fortune and all I needed was Evan Richards on YouTube. Anyhoo, it would have been stupid not to take advantage of Mal's good mood: "And is Lance going to be your fail-safe plan?" I asked. I'd been dying to know what had been said at the pub the other day.

"Hmm?"

"Your back-up plan." Mal always used to bang on about having a back-up plan. "You know, in case it doesn't work out with Gary."

"He wants to be my *main* plan. He said he realizes that I'm the girl for him."

"Wow! What did you say?"

"Jog on. But only after I let him know how inferior he was to Gary in *every* way. You don't go back to Turkey Twizzlers after you've had steak, do you?"

I couldn't think of a more perfect time to be rejected by ITV. What a relief!

The ITV building is a major contrast to Robert Fitzgerald's poky little office in Soho. It's a tall block on the South Bank of the Thames, near the London Eye. It's a big deal. I knew it. Malibu knew it. Unfortunately, my heart rate knew it too – it jumped a few hundred metres. Yikes! *Breathe*. In … out … in … out.

Malibu must have been able to tell. "Don't be nervous," she said kindly. *Perfect*, I thought. *If I begin to panic, remember Mal is now Buddha. It's all good.*

We announced ourselves at reception and then a woman with bobbed hair came and escorted us up to the boardroom. It was at the top of the building, with a view of London that tourists would pay a fortune for. You could see everything: the Shard, the Gherkin, Big Ben. Robert was already sitting at the meeting table, immaculately representing the silver foxes of this world. Beside him was a thirty-something male also in a suit.

"Malibu and Remy, please meet Peter Lonsdale."

We shook Peter's hand and he told us to take a seat.

"We're just waiting for the head of department," he explained.

There were eight empty chairs to choose from, so I looked at Malibu. Where should we sit? Away from them? Next to them? Was this some kind of test?

Malibu decided to sit facing them, and I slid into the chair next to her.

"Why don't you tell Peter a bit about yourselves, girls?"

Malibu began her patter... The British Kardashians... Footballer boyfriends... I stared at Peter, willing him to get on with it and tell her it wasn't going to work out. But he didn't. "Well, I'm sure Robert won't mind me revealing that we are very, very interested."

"Really?" Malibu chirped.

"*Very*. We're thinking ITV2. That's why the head of department wants to come across to meet you."

"He's a legend," put in Robert and then named five pro-grammes that the supposed legend was responsible for. All of them are in my top ten best shows ever, including: *I'm a Celeb*. But that wasn't the point. *This can't go any further*, I thought, *and I'm going to have to end it. NOW.*

"We love those shows, don't we Rem."

"Yes. But, um—"

"Ah! Here he is," said Peter.

An older man in a blue suit came into the room. He

had the whitest hair I'd ever seen. Peter stood up to introduce him.

"Remy and Malibu, please meet Tobias Berkley."

"Sorry for the delay, ladies. Lovely to meet you both."

When Tobias sat down, Robert asked Mal to talk about us, and how she saw the show working.

"I see what you mean," Tobias said to Robert when she'd finished, then turned to Mal. "You are an incredibly dynamic, young lady, Malibu."

Mal blushed. "Thank you."

"Now, let's back up for a moment. Your son – sorry, what did you say his name was?"

"Gary."

"Oh. But his father's called Gary as well, is that right?" Mal nodded. "Hmm. That could make things a bit tricky."

"Well, we just say Gary Junior for the baby."

"Yes, but that's far too complicated for our audience, who will be watching while they're tweeting, Facebooking, texting, Snapchatting – that's the latest thing, isn't it?"

"Got your finger on the pulse as always, Tobias," said Peter.

"I try," Tobias replied. "Anyway, I digress. Back to the baby problem. Does he have a nickname?"

"No."

"Not to worry, we can make one up. I'm supposing he has curly hair?"

"Quite curly, yes."

"Um… Curly Locks?" suggested Peter. And that sparked a nickname tennis match between the two of them as Malibu looked on in stone cold silence.

"Curly Wurly – that's it!" Tobias exclaimed.

"Fantastic," said Peter.

"Spot on," agreed Robert.

"But I've already thought of one that's much better," Malibu said.

Tobias raised his eyebrows. "What's that then?"

"*Gary Junior*. And if you don't want Gary Junior, quite frankly you can piss off."

She got up and stormed out.

"Erm… Well… I… Suppose that's it then?" I said to wrap it up.

It was. And Tobias ensured that we were escorted out by security!

When we got outside I turned to Malibu, majorly confused. "What happened? I thought you really wanted that show?"

"As Evan Richards says: 'Never compromise the things that are important to you and the right opportunity will come your way.' Once they started going on about Gary Junior I realized…"

"Wow. Yeah. You're right," I agreed. "And Mal, I need to be honest with you… I've been struggling for a long time. Fame doesn't suit me. That's why I've decided to move to Scotland."

"*Move to Scotland?* Why?"

"To be with Stephen."

She looked hurt at first. "When did you decide that?"

"A while ago," I admitted guiltily.

"You should have said something."

"I didn't want to let you down."

"I've been pushing hard, I admit. Must've been a nightmare to live with."

"Erm…" Was that a trick question?

"It's OK, you can admit it."

"A … little bit, yeah."

She smiled. "Rem… I'm so happy for you." And we were suddenly hugging in the middle of the pavement. "Told ya he'd ask you to live with him if you made out you were buying a flat."

"You were right – *as always*."

Evan Richards – I LOVE YOU!

10.30 p.m.

Just back from my interview at the Highland Manor. It went like a dream. I happily answered all the questions that the hotel's leisure manager threw at me. I even told her a few ideas of my own, like a Tanarama booth.

"Would there be much competition?" I checked.

"Naw, not near to us, anyway."

"Oh, I suppose Glasgow's inundated with spray-tan booths."

"Not nearly as much as you'd think."

"Uh-huh." ☺

On the taxi ride back to the airport, I had a chat with Camilla. She said she needed something to keep me in the mind of the celebrity booker for *Life Stories*. "I'm thinking that we set up a paparazzi photograph of you and Stephen looking at engagement rings."

"No thanks."

"Why not?"

"Stephen hasn't proposed."

"So?"

"*So* I'm not doing it! In fact, to quote my sister, I'm not doing anything that compromises the things that are important to me."

"But this would cement *Life Stories*."

"I don't care! Don't call me *ever* again, Camilla."

Thought it was the perfect day until I joined the queue to board the plane home and saw Angus bounding towards me. I'd forgotten he was going to Glasgow to see his new flat.

"We must be on the same flight," he boomed.

"Great."

The man standing behind me huffed at Angus for pushing in. So Angus glared at him, bodyguard style. "She's held the space for me, pal, *all right*?"

He wasn't about to argue with the man-mountain.

"Between you and me, the deal's done," Angus whispered in my ear.

"What deal?"

"You know. *The deal.*"

"Oh, you mean with—"

"Shush." He leant back in to whisper, "He's still got ter have a medical."

"Well, then it's not actually done, is it?" I said, a bit narked that Stephen had told him first.

The plane was full but Angus "negotiated" to swap seats with the man sitting beside me.

Gr–rrreat, I thought again.

"I never liked Rosie but I like yer, Remy," he said as he bounced into his seat.

"Erm … thanks."

"Yer know she used him, don't yer?"

"Angus, I don't really want to talk about—"

"So, yer need to understand what a big thing it was for Stevie when he said he'd look after yer."

Oh. Stephen must have been talking to him about us.

"Now, he knows yer *can* look after yerself. The point is he *wants* to look after yer. That's a big commitment. Especially after Rosie. Awkay?"

I nodded.

"And I'm happy fer yer both. Just…"

"Just what?"

"Well, we were a team, me and him. Yer know, Batman and Robin, Sherlock and Watson, Jazzy Jeff and The Fresh Prince. But he needs to get on with his new life now … look after him for me."

That was it – Angus handing his job over to me.

"I will. And thanks, Angus."

When we hit the London tarmac, I switched on my phone and had a text from a brand new Celtic player: *Deal agreed. Only medical left!* ☺

I texted back: *Woo-hoo! Love you, baby. I'm on the way.* xxx

I assumed I'd share a cab ride with Angus but he explained he was besotted with a girl who'd served him at the airport's Costa Coffee this morning, and he was going back to try his luck.

Stephen was making dinner when I got to his place. Risotto, which to be honest looked like sick.

"What do yer think?"

I had the perfect excuse. "Um… I'm not allowed to eat carbs, babe."

He took one spoonful and spat it out. "I can't eat that shite."

I said I'd make him some pasta. But there's a TV in the kitchen and I was distracted by *Friends* and boiled it to mush.

"The Big Man might have to come and live with us after all," he said.

Thursday 15 August – 10 a.m.

When we got into bed I said, "Baby, I've been thinking."

"Aw, that could be dangerous."

"I'm serious."

He started to stroke my hair. "Go on then."

"I'm sorry if I sounded ungrateful the other day. I just wanted you to know that I'm nothing like Rosie, so I don't want our relationship to be based on you looking after me. It should be based on both of us looking after each other."

"Sounds good to me."

"That's why I think we should go into business together."

He looked surprised.

"Open a salon, in Glasgow. You invest your money. I invest my skill and expertise. We split the profit fifty–fifty. What d'you think?"

"Who'll be the boss?" he said with a cheeky grin.

"Me. Obviously."

"Is that right?"

"Maybe we'll alternate then… Deal?"

"Whatever you say, Boss Lady," he said, swooping in for a kiss.

Stephen's gone to the airport now. He's flying to Glasgow to do his medical for Celtic. Before he left he said, "So, we're going into the salon business together?"

"Yep. But there's no hurry. If I get the spa job I'd like to take it – it'll be good research."

"Hmm…"

"What's up?"

"Just thinking… Campbell's Salon – has a nice ring to it."

I laughed. "We're a team, aren't we, babe?"

"Aye. At the top of the league." ☺

Saturday 7 September – 8 a.m.

Helloooo London!!!!!!

OK. I took an ickle diary break. But I am the salon manager at the Highland Manor and it's a v. big job!!!

Dr Clein would probably tell me off but guess what? I don't even need him anymore. He called to say he believed any further sessions would be a waste of money.

"Good luck, Remy, but I know you won't need it."

It's been full-on up in the Highlands, balancing the spa job with sorting out Lara's role at Tah-dah! plus looking for a house – all on a carb-free diet (which I hope to end in a few hours' time with an extra-large pizza with fries!!).

Today I'm in London for bikini photo-shoot day. And after that, it'll be the end of the hunger and grumpy, Feminazi-style salon managing. The end of my Terri Catalogue contract and the end of celebrity life. I can't wait!

So, when Harry phoned this morning to ask if I was sure I wanted to call it a day, I shrieked, "Blooming positive!" – though I may miss some of the perks, like Terri Catalogue putting me up in this swanky hotel, The May Fair.

I'm now about to phone Malibu. Stephen's flying down after his game and we're going to meet a few people for drinks in the hotel bar – Kellie, James, the Raymonds, NO Angus (funnily enough, the Raymonds insisted on that). So I'm asking Mal to bring Gary along too. They're getting on much better – she's stayed over at his house five times now. Mal's the one who cleared the air in the end. She told him she wants to be with him, but if he doesn't love her, she'll have to find a man who does because that's what she deserves.

"I'm a catch, aren't I, Rem? And if he doesn't see that, he can jog on."

"Evan Richards?" I guessed.

"No. You told me that – remember?"

"Oh, in that case, very wise words."

Anyhoo, it seems to have kicked Gary into gear. And whenever Mal gets nervous about him not taking her back for good, she chants. And for that we can thank Evan Richards. ☺

Sunday 8 September – 10 a.m.

WOW!!!!! What a great night!

I felt it was going to be good as soon as the bikini range photo shoot finished with Terry Neilson, the photographer, announcing "It's a wrap, guys."

"Woo-hoo!" I cheered.

That was swiftly followed by the grand closing of my Twitter account.

That's all folks! Been nice knowing ya. Peace. xxx

Then I tucked into the American Hot and fries I'd asked the assistant on the photo shoot to buy as soon as it was over. Carbs. I love carbs. And I have no intention of ever giving them up again.

As I was leaving, the Terri Catalogue representatives gave me a beautiful bunch of flowers as a thank you.

"No, thank *you,* guys," I said – I have a half-decent bank account because of them.

Headed back to my hotel like a Cheshire cat with double-thick cream. Could life get any better?

Yes, it bloody well could. Malibu turned up at The May Fair with Gary! We'd been in the bar for an hour by that time, so I was a bit merry. I'd just finished describing our cottage in Scotland to Suzy Raymond.

"Oh man, that sounds so awesome!" Suzy's the one who spotted Mal first. "Hey, isn't that your sister?"

I've known her for nineteen years and have never been so happy to see her in my life. Three weeks is a long time. We hugged each other tight.

"You look great, you skinny winnie," she said when we finally let go.

"Won't be skinny for long!" I said with a big smile on my face. "Want a drink?"

"Yeah. A Diet Coke for me."

"A what?!"

"Alcohol stops me being the *real* me."

OMG!

I got the barman's attention and ordered.

"How's it going, Remy?" asked Gary. *Nervously*, I thought.

"Fine," I said, semi ice queen. Didn't want to make it too easy for him.

"I'm sorry about how things were before you moved out," he said. "I intend to make it up to her."

"I hope so too." Frosty doesn't suit me. "It's really good to see you, Gary," I admitted. "Drink?"

When he walked off to say hello to Stephen and Oscar, I told Mal, "I'm glad he came. I've always liked him, you know. I just didn't like the way he was treating you."

"Neither did I."

"How's it going anyway?"

"Chanting works. That's all I'm saying." Methinks the wink that followed spoke volumes!

Gary was proper drunk by the end of the night. To be honest, all of us were except Malibu, but she's happy on air these days!! She threw her arms up and danced to EVERY-THING the DJ played. By 3 a.m., the Raymonds had gone home for some beauty sleep, James and Dominic had gone off for a curry, Kellie had pulled and there was only Stephen, Gary, myself and Malibu left.

"We'd better go to bed," I slurred.

"You staying here?" Gary slurred back. "I'd love to see your room – heard they're great in this place."

"Aye. They're pretty good," McFit managed to say.

I thought asking to see our room was a bit strange but was too tipsy to debate. "Sure. Come on up."

They both followed us to the lift and as we stood waiting for it to arrive, Gary suddenly got down on one knee!!!!

I've never seen Mal turn as red as she did then. "Gary, what are you doing?"

"Malibu Bennet. You are a good woman. Not perfect, but a good, good woman. I do not want to lose you again so … will you do me the honour of marrying me?"

She went even redder. "You're drunk, Gary. Get up."

"Yes, I'm drunk. I am *velly* drunk – but I want to marry you. And I will not get up until you say yes."

The lift arrived and the doors opened. I stepped in and pressed the hold button. Stephen followed.

"Um, Mal… We're waiting," I said with a grin.

"I will stay here, on this knee. No matter how long it takes," Gary promised.

"OK then, yes," Mal said, with tears in her eyes. "Yes, you bloody idiot. Now get up."

Woo-hoo!

I am Remy Louise Bennet. I'm a work in progress, and I may not be perfect. But I blooming well love my life!

Acknowledgements

With thanks to:
KT Forster
Helen McAleer
Gill Evans
Emma Lidbury
Annalie Grainger
Claire Sandeman
Jo Humphreys-Davies and the marketing team
Kate Beal
Sean Moss
Maria Soler Canton
Jas Chana and everyone at Mobcast
Mark Hodgson and BlackBerry
Ruth Harrison and The Reading Agency
Caroline Odland
Tim Holloway

Want MORE drama?!

Then you'll love these books too! ☺ →

Love
R x

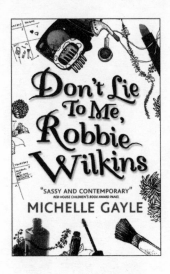

OMG! My bum looks *huge* in this LBD!

Minutes away from a date with Robbie Wilkins.
Him: The buffest Premiership footballer around.
Me: Now officially an elephant. ☺

I can't believe I snogged him on my
17th-and-a-half birthday! (He's a proper catch.)

Kellie says I should tell him my salon business
plans: not just BEAUTIFUL but ambitious too. ☺

This is gonna be an amaaaaaazing year...

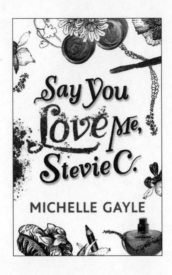

I, Remy Louise Bennet, need to re-evaluate my life...

Am v. successful salon owner,
aka Boss Lady. GOOD

Will soon be an auntie (woo-hoo!!) GOOD
Malibu (mum-to-be) has a *small*
"Who's the daddy?" problem. Hmm. BAD

Have new, improved McFitty boyfriend. GOOD
But will he cheat on me too...? BAD

Result: Must take "pre-emptive action" (read that in top business mag, ha-ha ☺)

Bring it on...

This year I will find FULL-ON, LONG-TERM L O V E.

I will also take it upon myself to help Gran with her iPad so she doesn't end up a global laughing stock. She can have the ANGRY BIRDS app and THAT'S IT!

And finally, I, **Hattie Moore,** will officially get to know my REAL DAD. After last year, I really have to. Even if he does think recycling baked bean tins is more important than his long lost daughters! W H A T E V E R – this year is going to be totally **AMAZEBALLS!**

HANNAH is smart and funny.
She's also fifteen and pregnant.

AARON is the new boy at school.
He doesn't want to attract attention.

So why does Aaron offer to be the
pretend dad to Hannah's unborn baby?